RIAL INDUSTRIAL IND
E   ESTATE   E

RIAL INDUSTRIAL IND
E   ESTATE   E

DUSTRIAL   INDUSTRI
ESTATE   ESTATE

DUSTRIAL   INDUSTRI
ESTATE   ESTATE

The work of editing *Industrial Estate* takes place on the stolen land and waterways of Gadigal Country. We pay our deepest respects to Elders, past and present. We extend warmth and solidarity to Aboriginal and Torres Strait Islander peoples across the continent. Gadigal Country, as well as the numerous lands on which the words within *Industrial Estate* were written and printed, were never ceded, sold or given up. May justice, truth and treaties prevail. May liberation and Land Back be known in our lifetimes.

Always was, always will be Aboriginal land.

Industrial Estate
Writing from the working class
Issue 1

First published 2024
by Subbed In
www.subbed.in

Cover artwork of bird adapted from *Common Buzzard* (1837) by Robert Havell (engraver)
after John James Audubon (artist), featured in *The Birds of America* (Plate CCCLXXII), Public Domain,
courtesy National Gallery of Art, Washington, under Creative Commons Zero (CC0 1.0 Universal)

Pages 10-11: *Big Fish Eat Little Fish* by Pieter Bruegel (1556) engraved by Pieter van der Heyden (1557),
courtesy The Met under Creative Commons Zero (CC0)

Pages 26-129: All artwork by Giovanni Battista Bracelli from the series *Bizzarie di varie Figure* (1624),
Public Domain, courtesy National Gallery of Art, Washington, under Creative Commons Zero (CC0 1.0 Universal)

Book and cover design: Dan Hogan
Editors: Victoria Manifold and Dan Hogan
Proofreader/copyeditor: Hollen Singleton

Text set in Domaine Text

A catalogue record for this book is available from the National Library of Australia

ISBN: 978-0-6451524-1-8

Website: www.subbed.in
X: @subbedin
Instagram: @subbedin
Facebook: www.facebook.com/subbedinsydney
Email: hello@subbed.in

INDUSTRIAL ESTATE

issue 1

WRITING FROM THE WORKING CLASS

EDITORIAL

DAN HOGAN & VICTORIA MANIFOLD

We write this editorial on unceded Gadigal Country, 236 years since the commencement of colonial invasion. As we write, the colony's Labor–Liberal political establishment continues to enrich Israeli apartheid and genocide with its contracts, with its trade ties, with its supportive rhetoric, with its obfuscation of its own complicity in the atrocities committed against Palestinians, with its obsequious diplomacy, and with its attacks on people of conscience who stand for the liberation of Palestine.

All over the continent people are being silenced and punished for taking action for Palestine, and writers and artists are no exception. Public institutions, such as libraries, broadcasters and universities, have enacted draconian measures to suppress, demonise and disrupt pro-Palestine speech and organising. Like a fish, the Labor–Liberal political establishment rots from the head down and the threat of even more extreme suppression at the hands of the state looms large as the duopoly continues its march further and further right.

Labor–Liberal anti-democracy ideology is in lockstep with the 'like-minded' states at the imperial core with whom it claims moral alignment. This active alignment includes the UK whose arts council recently threatened to withdraw funding from artists whose work 'might be considered overtly political or activist'. In response, writer and translator Jen Calleja tweeted: 'Easier said than done but take all the art away from funders. DIY it, keep it small, among ourselves, anything to be able to have freedom of expression for things like calling out genocide, calling out fascism. Why do you think I/we chose to make art?'

So this is our answer. *Industrial Estate* is a project that rejects capitalist meritocracy and refuses to abide ruling class decorum. And it is in the spirit of refusal that solidarity is forged. It is in solidarity that we say, with our full chests, from the river to the sea, always was, always will be.

But it is not just the job of the working class to refuse; it is incumbent on people anywhere and of all classes to take action against injustice everywhere. Cowardice is a systemic rot that plagues all classes in service of the ruling class, in service of colonialism and capitalism.

We call upon readers to stand in solidarity with anti-colonial, anti-capitalist struggle. As working-class people we don't have the capital or connections of our upper-class counterparts but we will always have solidarity, and solidarity is forever. If publishing and funding opportunities are contingent on silence in the presence of injustice, then these are not opportunities at all. They are containment measures designed to stifle solidarity. We will refuse this containment and DIY it instead, all the while saying: Palestine will be free. And Palestine will free us all. Long live Palestine.

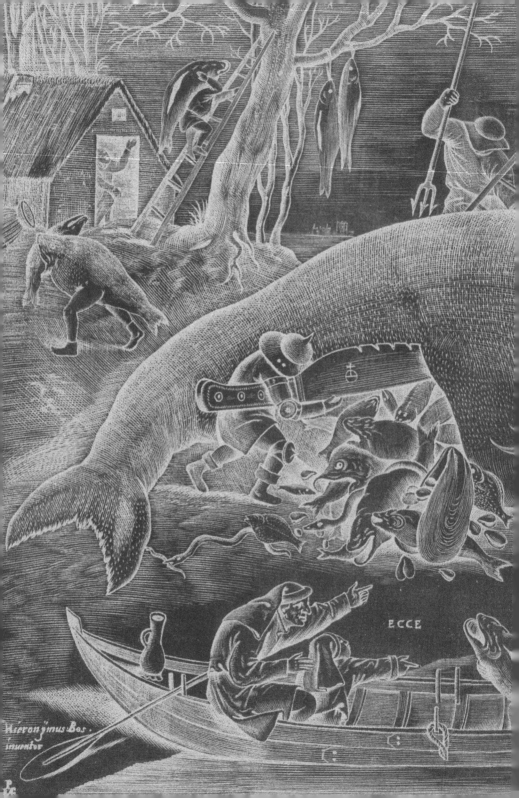

ECCE

Hieronymus Bos.
inventor

CORK EXCV 1557

A SECURE BUILDING IS THE FOUNDATION FOR A BETTER FUTURE

EMMA RAYWARD

Emma Rayward recently completed her PhD with a thesis titled, *Topological Urban Novel (Completely Normal and Perfectly Regular)* at the Writing and Society Research Centre of Western Sydney University. She writes science fiction that is concerned with state infrastructure, bureaucratic language and community resistance. She was raised on Birpai land and now lives on Gadigal land.

I nhabitants of the Nation are defined as members of the Nation who have a residence within the Nation. A residence of the Nation is defined as a room or set of rooms within a building, a building, or a set of buildings contained within any neighbourhood or neighbourhood system of the Nation, which is permanently or temporarily occupied by an inhabitant of the Nation.

To be considered an inhabitant of the Nation, a member must have been born in the Nation. There are members of the Nation who were not born in the Nation, because they were not born at all. To be born means to be produced as a discrete set within the body of a member of the Nation, and then expelled from this body into the Nation. Producing a new member does not destroy the topology of the body, as no new holes are created or closed.

There are members of the Nation who were born in the Nation that are not homeomorphic to inhabitants of the Nation. These members are of a different class to inhabitants of the Nation and are themselves comprised of a number of non-equivalent classes. There is no common language between inhabitants of the Nation and members of the Nation who are not homeomorphic to inhabitants of the Nation. There may be no common language between any members of non-equivalent classes, but inhabitants of the Nation cannot confirm this.

To occupy a residence, and therefore be considered an inhabitant of the Nation, a member must be employed in the Nation, be a dependent of an inhabitant employed in the Nation, or be actively looking for employment in the Nation. Some residences within the Nation may be assigned to inhabitants depending on the type of employment the inhabitant participates in. Some residences may be occupied by reason of a transfer of payments from one inhabitant to another inhabitant, or from one inhabitant to the Nation. The value of the payment has a correlation with the number of rooms, the location, the quality of the building materials, and its level of upkeep, though it may not be a one-to-one correlation. The desirability of any one residence affects its position within the market of total residences.

There are members of the Nation who were born in the Nation and are homeomorphic to inhabitants of the Nation but are not considered inhabitants of the Nation as they do not have a residence within the Nation due to their employment status. These members may be unable to look for employment or may have no other inhabitant on which they can be dependent. Every inhabitant of the Nation has a residence in the Nation, but not every residence in the Nation has an inhabitant who occupies it. While there may be unoccupied residences, members of the

Nation who are homeomorphic to inhabitants of the Nation but do not have a residence, may not be permitted to occupy them, as they are unemployed, are unable to look for employment, or have no other inhabitant upon which they can be dependent.

□□□□□□□□□□□□□□□□□

There exists a set of inhabitants who own a greater number of buildings than the complement set of inhabitants, in an attempt to occupy greater space. While an inhabitant may own a greater number of discrete rooms, the total volume of these rooms may not necessarily be greater than a single room owned by any other inhabitant. To maximise the chance for greater volume, some inhabitants purchase more and more rooms, more and more buildings. Volume, however, does not guarantee the quality of the space.

Ownership of buildings in the Nation is contentious. Some inhabitants, typically those who do not own any buildings, do not consider buildings to be ownable, given that buildings have the capacity to exist independently of inhabitants, and by extension, can anything really be owned? Other inhabitants, typically those who do own buildings, argue that, well, buildings were built, were given life, as it were, by inhabitants and therefore could and should be owned. The non-building-owning class of inhabitants question this logic. Do inhabitants not also give life to other inhabitants, are these inhabitants then owned? Would it not be better to establish more of a caretaker role? The building-owning class of inhabitants consider this to be an illogical comparison, and, if they were caretakers, should they not receive adequate compensation for this? Plus, in many instances, it was through the investment of the building-owning class of inhabitants that new buildings were constructed, so rightfully they should have control over them. The non-building-owning class argued, okay, so what about builders? It may have been your investment, but it was not your labour. If this is what you are basing your ownership on, should builders not then own, or at least partially own, the buildings they build? And what of the materials used? If you consider yourselves to have given buildings life, you did not give life to the materials from which the building was constructed. These materials also have the capacity to exist independently of inhabitants. To which the property-owning class of inhabitants replied, okay, first of all, builders have been adequately compensated for their labour, and yes, maybe the materials from which the building is constructed have the capacity to exist independently of inhabitants, but it is the union of such materials that is unique. Without builders, and the investment of the building-owning class, these materials would not have come together to make a building in which, by the way, you, the non-building-owning class, have been permitted to live. The non-building-owning class wonders, could these materials not come together to make a building independently of inhabitants? Have they been given any such chance?

The building-owning class of inhabitants does not understand why the non-building-owning class of inhabitants are not more grateful for being permitted to live in a building that is owned by a member of the building-owning class. They do not have the responsibility of building maintenance, they can happily live in this building without worry. Yes, some may consider it a right to have a place of residence inside a building, but that does not mean it should be given for free. Someone must pay for it, and why should it not be the inhabitant who is residing there? Why should it be a member of the building-owning class, when they themself do not reside in the building under question? If every inhabitant owned a building, how would new buildings ever be built? It is fine, actually, that there are empty buildings, because their existence supports the competitiveness of the market of buildings, a market which, really, needs to see constant growth. Is not growth an indicator of health? And is not health the priority of the Nation? One could argue, the building-owning class argues, that the building-owning class are more like doctors, tending to the health of the Nation by ensuring its growth.

□□□□□□□□□□□□□□□□□

An inhabitant is employed, or they are not. Even if an inhabitant is employed, they may also be under-employed, under-designating not enough employment, and therefore income, is received by an inhabitant in relation to the cost of living in the Nation. An under-employed inhabitant may be more fortunate than an unemployed inhabitant, assuming that an unemployed inhabitant is actually in need of the income received by said employment, as there may also be unemployed inhabitants who are not in need of income generated by employment as income is bestowed upon them by those they are dependent on, that is, if an inhabitant, or set of inhabitants related to the unemployed inhabitant, known as a family or a collection, have amassed fat stacks of cash, capital, assets, or numbers indicating such, which is then shared with the unemployed inhabitant, sometimes in exchange for a title, as in, the unemployed inhabitant is given a portion of the aforementioned stacks while acting as a consultant, for example, for an organisation under the control of a member of their family. Perhaps, also, an unemployed inhabitant of the Nation may be of a young or old age, and thus necessarily dependent on another inhabitant, and therefore not capable, or considered capable, of acting in any position of employment.

An under-employed inhabitant is not necessarily working less, or less hard, but the under- designates the insufficiency of their income corresponding to the living cost of the Nation. The Nation says, maybe if you move to a less dense neighbourhood of the Nation, you will succeed in gaining a level of employment that is not under-, to which an under-employed inhabitant replies, how do I move to a less dense neighbourhood of the Nation, exactly? An inhabitant who may be unemployed, and for whatever reason does not require employment, may repeat this sentiment, saying to the unemployed or under-employed inhabitants, it is not that hard. Look at me, I can get by just fine, so you obviously can. Just get employment. Just go out and get it.

For the chronically unemployed, a residence, along with other necessities, is provided, up to a point. If an inhabitant has been actively looking for employment for six months but has not, in that time, participated in any form of employment, then they are deemed no longer actively looking for employment. During this six-month period, the unemployed inhabitant is required to participate in activities as set out by the Nation, as a way of earning the residence. This may include participating in activities for which there is no income, and proving, in periods of two weeks, that they are actively looking for employment. This is considered by the Nation as a mutual obligation, where one party provides residence and other necessities, and the other party proves that they are attempting to provide these things for themselves. That the period of reporting attempts to gain employment is two weeks is arbitrary. That an inhabitant is given six months to find employment is arbitrary.

Surely it is the case that, after six months of actively looking for employment, an inhabitant would have found something, anything? An inhabitant who has not found any employment after six months is being too picky, probably, at which point is it not only fair and right that they no longer be provided residence? Why should they be a burden on other inhabitants of the Nation, who are themselves employed?

If an inhabitant who has not been engaged in any employment for six months does not have another inhabitant, one who is employed, that they can become dependent on, then, unfortunately, there is simply no residence available to them. In this case, an inhabitant is no longer considered an inhabitant of the Nation, they become only a member.

◻◻◻◻◻◻◻◻◻◻◻◻◻◻◻◻◻

It is necessary that inhabitants of the Nation move amongst buildings, as a residence and workplace of any one inhabitant may not exist within the same building or the same neighbourhood. The residence and workplace of an inhabitant may not be near each other at all. The Nation is aware of the complexities that may arise as a result of such a commute and has put in place limited plans to mitigate this. Despite this general awareness, workplaces do not often make any further accommodations for movement between buildings. Workplaces associated with the Nation may offer greater allowances than workplaces not associated with the Nation, though this is not guaranteed, and it may never be sufficient for every employee. Such allowances include, but are not limited to: a period of travel time included in the total hours of the work day, paid or unpaid; a time-in-lieu system, where an employee is able to work additional hours on other days in order to accrue travel time that may be then used when necessary; capacity for remote work if the type of work allows it, or alternatively, access to devices which allow work while commuting; opportunity for residence within the same neighbourhood, or the same building, as the workplace.

The Nation has mandated that no workplace is permitted to terminate an employee immediately if they are late due to difficulties moving between buildings in the Nation, they must first attempt to mitigate the lateness. Only if the methods a workplace applies does not have any positive impact on the punctuality of the employee in question, then the workplace is permitted to terminate their employment.

Workplaces may be reluctant to offer additional allowances to their employees who, if given the opportunity, will then demand more and more until the workplace has nothing left to give, at which point it may not be profitable for the workplace to remain functioning and so must cease operations, leaving all employees unemployed. For this outcome, of course only employees would be to blame, by demanding so much from their workplaces. Employees may argue with their employer as to the fairness of such blame, saying that they are not in control of the location of buildings within the Nation, so should not both parties at least be equally responsible? The employer responds to such questions with questions of their own. Would it not be responsible to allow maximum time to get to work, as in, to leave earlier? Would it not be responsible to move to a neighbourhood that was near the neighbourhood which contains the workplace? Would it not be responsible to move to the same neighbourhood as the workplace? To which the employees reply, okay but to where, to which building exactly? Just how early should we leave for work, should we never go home? Should we just work or be travelling to and from work every hour of every day? And the employers answer, yes. If that is what it takes. They refuse to take any more questions.

Employees ask, to anyone who will listen, would it not

be responsible for employers to restructure workplaces, to alter business models to best suit the function of the Nation, the Nation that it is known to be difficult to navigate, and thus provide a supportive environment in which employees can work? Is not sleep and free time necessary to optimal functioning in the workplace? Other employees, from other workplaces, listen and say, yes, it would be, yes, it is. But none of these employees have yet the capacity to restructure any workplace, so nothing changes.

□□□□□□□□□□□□□□□□

Suppose that an employer offers an employee a residence within the same building as the workplace. The only travel necessary is then contained within the building itself, from one room to another room, whether it be on the same or different level. Suppose that this employer is not associated with the Nation, and so to offer a residence within the same building as the workplace requires the employer to have control over other rooms within the building, and that said rooms be available.

Suppose that all other rooms within the building under consideration are occupied by inhabitants who are not employees of the workplace. The employer may offer these inhabitants compensation for vacating these rooms. This compensation may or may not be fair and may or may not be only a suggestion. The employer may adopt other tactics to encourage the inhabitants to rescind their occupation of the rooms that it desires to repopulate, through noise, excessive lights, or other kinds of disruptive action. Suppose that a number of the inhabitants succumb to the pressure to vacate the residence. These inhabitants will need to then secure other rooms, in other buildings, in the same or other neighbourhoods.

EMMA RAYWARD

Such a move may or may not be beneficial for their own travel to work. An inhabitant in this situation may have no choice but to move into a building of lower quality, one that may even require a greater fee for inhabitation.

Suppose that an inhabitant an employer is persuading to leave the building is themselves an employee of a different workplace that is also located in the building, an employee that the other workplace holds in high value, and intends to protect from the predatory actions from their rival employer. This second employer may engage in their own tactics to deter the first employer: they may alter the methods of access into the building, may restrict access to sources of energy, and may also use noise and light disturbance. The employers behaving in such a way to push the other out of the building creates a wholly unliveable building for every inhabitant, inhabitants that may or may not be employed by either of the workplaces. Repairs may remain unattended, waste products may build up. Both employers may use an excessive package of capital and resources to push the employees of their opponent out, to the detriment of their original purpose. The building becomes uninhabitable, both workplaces collapse. Inhabitants lose their residences and employees lose their workplaces.

Employers may simply move on and establish new workplaces elsewhere, but as a result, are unlikely to offer such generous offers of assistance to employees in the future, citing the consequences of their own action as solely the fault of the employee. If the employees just allowed extra travel time to get to their workplace each day, then they would not need to be moved into the same building as the workplace, and if they did not need to be moved into the same building as the workplace, the employer would then not have needed to expend the massive number of resources securing the new residence that was obviously necessary. If the employees just allowed extra travel time to get to their workplace each day, then the workplace would have not failed, and every employee would be able to retain their positions. If you want everyone to retain their positions, the employers say to the employees, you will be at the workplace on time.

□□□□□□□□□□□□□□□

If you are not at work on time, you will become unemployed. If you are unemployed, you will no longer have a residence. If you do not occupy a residence, you cannot be an inhabitant of the Nation. If you are not an inhabitant of the Nation, you can only be a member of the Nation. An inhabitant of the Nation and a member of the Nation are not equivalent, and thus, do not experience equivalency in the Nation. These are the conditions that define the Nation, these immutable, perfect conditions around which the Nation is organised. They cannot be changed.

Nothing changes but stress grows, nothing changes but dissatisfaction grows, nothing changes but frustration grows, nothing changes but anger grows. When such emotions grow, can it truly be said that nothing changes? Stress and dissatisfaction and frustration and anger become growths that eke out into the Nation, cover buildings, and infest foundations, eating away at the material which gives a building its shape. The growths become their own buildings, threatening to overrun the Nation, and perhaps they erect a new Nation in its place.

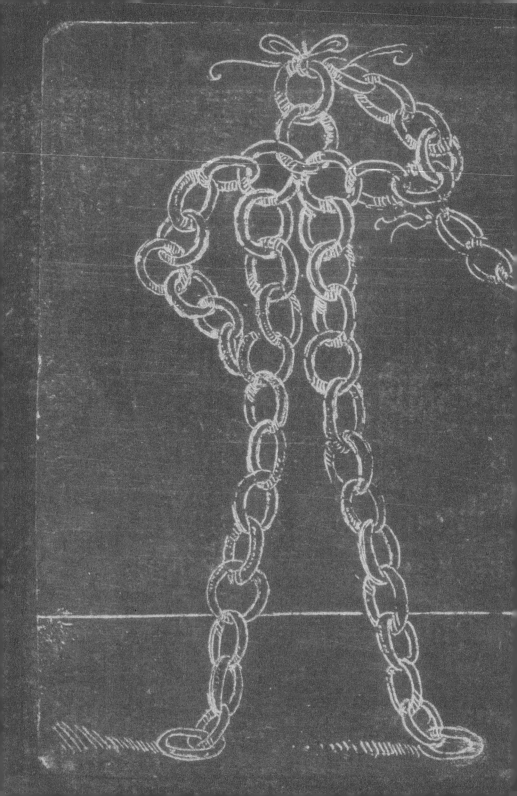

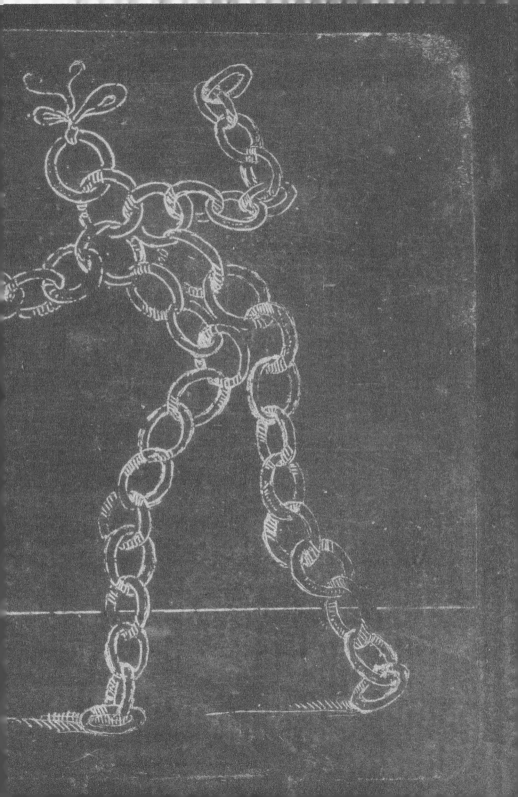

2 POEMS

LUCY NORTON

Lucy Norton is a storyteller of Koori and Quechua heritage living and creating on Gadigal land. Her work explores themes of ancestral heritage, connection and lived experience. They're a recipient of the Varuna First Nations Fellowships 2023, Red Room Emerging Poets Residency 2024 and their work has been published by Red Room Poetry, *kindling & sage* and *Right Now Magazine*.

dead dad altar

i am thinking about your birthday
on monday, nearly seventy but
gone longer than alive to me

i am slowly putting washing on the line
thinking of how you are still close by
in the pool of life we both swim

i am thinking about leaving you an offering
slice up some woolies mud cake for your birthday
roll you up a cigarette for christmas lunch

i am quickly putting washing on the line
so i can run inside, write this down
it is very hot and the clothes will dry soon

sky talk

i am five years old singing
a television theme song
to my dying father

we go back home
with aunt and unc
i watch roaches
dance on the ceiling
wondering if they
have fathers too

cracks in the wall
to keep me company
paternal face in
a velvet curtain

they tell me

```
        *              you
  *               live
        in              *
  *               the
sky                     *
        now
          *
```

i attach notes to balloons
but you never write back

REVIEW

DAVID STAVANGER

David Stavanger is a poet, producer, parent and lapsed psychologist living on Dharawal land. He is the co-editor of *Admissions: Voices Within Mental Health* (Upswell, 2022) and his most recent collection is *Case Notes* (UWAP, 2020).

Real estate agent sends me a new lease || with a larger increase than prior years || I suggest a halfway place || where we can meet in the middle || of their increased costs || servicing a Lexus || branded gym gear || and my decreasing faith || in secure future housing || the outsourcing of angels || the lease has both landlords listed || investment couple || so I look them up online || they're on a podcast || talking about buying 9 properties || in 15 months || in that same period || I ate approximately 51 Coles croissants || have much gravitas to show for it || one of their websites is about building empires || selling things people want to buy || like ads for clients || anything platinum || conceptual coins || and the biggest life lessons || that it's not easy to turnaround a cruise ship || that there's a good reason || niche rhymes with rich || which it doesn't || but who am I to correct || he provides off-shore staffing solutions || I find a post of theirs on socials || about passing government taxes onto tenants || which makes it sound like a baton || as if we're in the same race || as if we're both really living || under the same roof || and I will get to cross the line || between us || their main childhood recollection || seems to be about imported products || lessons learnt in their twenties || that a party is all about the numbers || and money never gets old || I am getting older || prefer small gatherings || the main thing I learnt in my twenties || is that people like them || will always take the last beer || from your fridge

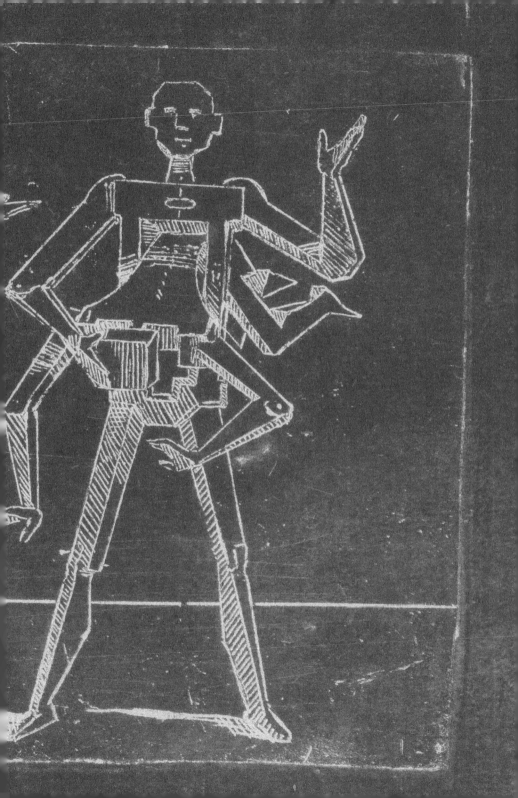

THEY ARE MOSS

HOLLEN SINGLETON

Hollen Singleton is a writer/editor and teaches at the University of Melbourne. They live in Sunshine on Wurundjeri Land.

Mum keeps calling it *mould*, take as much *mould* as you want, there's always more *mould*. I'm scraping moss from the parking lot of a caravan park where my parents work. It seems funny to me: a category confusion. Moss is, unlike mould, *intensely vital*. It beams with significance, to the collector, to the zealot. Peels of it come away from the gravel and into my plastic container.

In a single bank of moss—in a rainforest, of course, forming a photogenic wall pointed to and petted by hikers, glistening with dew, but also found along the untended, open-air ramp to a train station, or on a rotting log, and in the dankest corner of the backyard, a collection point for run-off, probably totally full of toxic substances and waste, excreta possibly—there are many separate plants. Mosses is grammatically correct. I use the words *moss* and *mosses* interchangeably, apologies to Robin Wall Kimmerer, the expert that brought this world under a microscope for many, myself included. She is extremely clear on the multiplicity of mosses: 'the "moss" is many different mosses, of widely divergent forms.' Mosses live in clumps, but that clustering is a composition of genetically distinct, non-vascular plants, each clinging with its rhizoid. A carpet of mosses—plural always—may cohere to create a superstructure: the forest fairyland, the untidy hillock in the backyard niche, the scum to be scraped from the train station at regular intervals—or ransacked from the caravan park parking lot.

This is solidarity: a speck reaching towards the clump, which may also be composed of specks.

In *Gathering Moss*, Kimmerer writes, 'Moss plants almost never occur singly, but in colonies packed as dense as an August cornfield [...] Separated from the rest of a clump, an individual moss shoot dries immediately.' I've covered the book in post-its and drawn on it with green pen. It's not the only book on mosses, but yes, it is. That is to say, it's fantastic. Do you want to care about moss? Start here. Make room in your heart.

I've bought a magnifying glass called a loupe. It's barely bigger than a fifty-cent piece and I'm going to put it on my lanyard. My ex-girlfriend informs me that this would be devastating for my vibes. Mary Douglas writes in *Purity and Danger*, 'Dirt is matter out of place.' Mould is moss out of place.

Non-vascular means they don't have the same system for stretching out like trees or other plant life. They don't have the veins to carry what they need, primarily water, up to their leaves once they get taller than about 10cm. This is why they remain on the surface and are the surface, working their miniature root networks into whatever they're astride.

You might see the sporophyte: the flying tendril that lifts out of the carpet of moss with its seedpod cap. These are their tallest constructions, trying to catch some air, trying to find an airborne moment to go forth and multiply.

Bryophytes, the first to crawl up from the primordial water, have made it global: mosses, liverworts, hornworts. Mosses reproduce variably. They can reproduce through mites, infinitesimal and visually unappealing LIFE, through coatings of sperm, if it must be called that. Mosses survive flooding and drought, can enter a pseudo-death at will; this death being only a slowing of metabolic processes, a quiet quitting. Their societies rise and fall with floodlines, and flow over each other and slough off their surfaces, the surfaces that are them, rhizoidally inflected surfaces, say of a log, that can slough off, spreading moss sperm, spreading water that holds these tiny swimmers, or creating new clones—no sperm, only spores—depending on the sexual/asexual nature of the moss of that kind, in that place, in that time. They're replicators, lifting their millions of sporophytes up, cupped in a capsule. They're trans, sometimes, some of them, depending on anything and everything else.

I order a punnet of sustainable mosses over eBay. It arrives in a package, wet to the touch—of course it would be wet. This cannot have been good in the hand of the postie. There has been a damaging journey to my door: damaging to my post, damaging to the post of others. Yet when I open it, there isn't a tendril out of place. They, the mosses, sit in a paper dish, looking like a succulent takeaway meal. They are perfect in the packaging, fronds overlapping, touching each other, no gaps, no sense of mosses out of the moss. If I had placed it in a terrarium, under glass and devoid of *conditions* of any kind, maybe this could have been preserved. Once I scatter it, rehoming it here and there, the effect dematerialises. The god-like intentionality gone. *Is this gardening?* I try to embed chunks of it in the dankest part of my yard, around which the landlord has laid a concave divot of concrete, ignoring the swampy quality of the earth beneath.

My rental house is going to fall down and get eaten by lichen, moss, hornworts. In my dreams.

Lichen, Mould and Moss On Roofs: What To Do About It.

A clean roof is a thing of beauty ... While moss doesn't have real roots, it has tiny protrusions that look like roots, and it will form its own soil by collecting dirt and debris from the air.

Ever had an enemy? Your roof and concrete does — moss.

If we were not around, moss would break apart our streets and structures.

Gathering Moss.

Allegedly, the moss rhizoids penetrate tiny cracks in the shingles and accelerate their deterioration ... there is no scientific evidence to support or refute this claim ... [It seems] that a mossy roof represents a hint of moral decay.

Jenny Offill begins her smash-hit novel *Weather* with possession:

Notes from a town meeting in Milford, Connecticut, 1640:
Voted, that the earth is the Lord's
and the fullness thereof; voted,
that the earth is given to the Saints;
voted, that we are the Saints.

It says that we are responsible for what happens here, in this context, that is Earth. Here, Earth is decapitalised, 'earth', dirt. Is it saying *earth* like *land*, the way that very old texts didn't need to think further than the tracts of land they could see from the back of a stout pony?

How to resonate with sainthood as responsibility when I am a speck, dirty, part of the uncountable noun that is e/Earth.

Mosses multiply when it suits them. When they can, they reproduce sexually. They need: water, weather, to be touched by cryptozoa—crypto-zoa, *secret animals*, half the size of fleas, creatures that live in darkness, damp and decomposition. These are affiliations and contingencies, options.

There's still more: if the wind vibrates the sporophyte, a hair-thin tendril with a head full of spores, and if it, the wind, churns just right, not just blows straight but blows wild and turbulent, the spores, millions, then release and scatter. They make more of their same thing, again.

I disperse the chunks of moss from the caravan park and the eBay punnet along my front yard, edging the trail I've made in the yard around the oleander. The trail is for my bins. My bins travel it once a week, kicking up the shreds of mosses I've hand-dug into the ground and willed to survive. What am I doing with mosses, making a woodland? I take tree trunk slices too, from a construction site, and *strew* them. This is texture.

Some of the mosses dig in, networking with the mediocre soil, earth that remembers the factories in the west, asbestos rain and the everyday heavy metals. Where I live used to be Maribyrnong swampland. My possessive bones insist that this be true, that the mosses belong here, that I am a saint. This should grow *here*. This is their place.

The bin wheels kick them up and I dig them back down again. Sporophytes rise, like the heads of prey animals looking for a predator, and under my loupe they look healthy and ready to go.

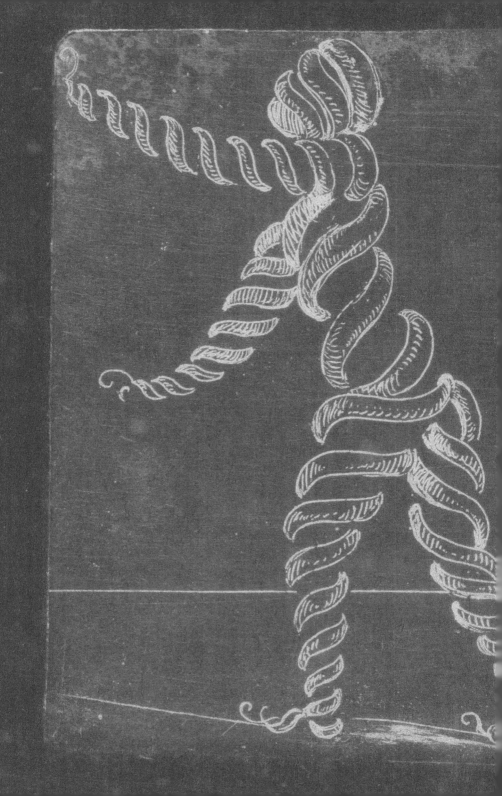

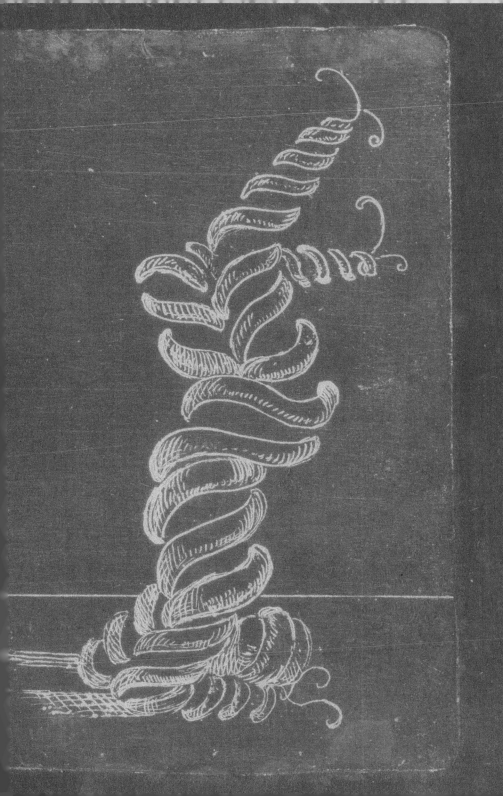

IN A VACUUM

NATALIA FIGUEROA BARROSO

Natalia Figueroa Barroso is a writer of Uruguayan origins living on Dharug Country. Natalia is a member of Sweatshop Literacy Movement, and her work has appeared in *Griffith Review, Meanjin, Overland* and more. Natalia is currently working on her debut novel, *Hailstones Fell without Rain* (2025, UQP). She posts at @ms_figueroa_barroso

over the professional vacuum cleaner,
my lil sis & i fight.
every single graveyard shift
we play electrical cord tug-of-war
while i imagine the other kids in our hood, fairfield west, where we live, go to bed
because it's late at night & no one under 14 works but us.
the fighting drives mamá loca. "¡basta gurisas!" she says
as she feather dusts keyboards & pcs in all the ways.
fake blonde curls in a tight bun like her bank account. at least
the dust glistens under the insect-infested fluorescent lights, a feast
for our rumbling-hungry ocean blue eyes,
in the office ceiling of skies.

the bulky vacuum straps to my back like my school bag.
i know my next confession may make me a bigtime dag
but it brings me pride
that despite its heaviness i can still support its hefty weight.
even as scrawny as i am,
we (the vacuum & i) somehow workout, like it's fate.
like aircons & western sydney summers are predestined for one another.
or how a fast-beat merengue song & a cleaning gig seem to go together.

NATALIA FIGUEROA BARROSO

emptying its bag is gross though.
dust particles go up my lil sis & i's nostrils
& make us cough & sneeze out clear snot, which of course we wipe
onto our green two-sizes-too-small school jumper sleeves. but more
unpleasant is the knotted hair that gets stuck in its metal tube. in all colours. blond,
brown, black. odd because most of the employees
at the amp office in westie skyscraper parra, where we work, are grey-haired balding men
in white collar shirts & navy tailored suits.

i know this because
i often grab their blinding silver-framed family portraits
on their desks.
where they're dressed in their best. blue ties around their necks
that hide under their
double chins. gold watches matching their thick
wedding bands. with their barbie-dolled wives & blue-eyed children by their side.
although, my familia and their family both have blue eyes,
ours reflect off hotel pissed-in pools, cleaned by latinas like my mamá.
theirs, however, are posing for us, shimmering like a sun kissed ocean
promoting their luxurious lives
like the billboards on the m4 which display flights
to unaffordable & unattainable destinations.

mamá makes us take turns with the vacuum as she
empties overfilled rubbish bins & scrubs poo-stained toilets & mops away debt.
meanwhile, the vacuum roars

over the harsh words my lil sis & i say to ourselves,
the ones that make us feel inadequate. or worthless.
the: youse losers, youse povos, youse gronks, youse wogs.
because its orange cord is infinite like our imagination. & within seconds
its extended metallic pipe transforms into a
salsa dance partner. swivelling its plastic feet from side to side
while we sway our hips in all the ways like mamá does with her feather duster.

its red buttons switch into all the ones we can't push
at home. or as we walk the
streets of fairfield. or as mamá complains about abuela meddling.
or when abuela's gossiping about mamá & her lack of cooking from scratch
to her neighbour while they water their daisies & a single petal falls, disappearing with
the metallic-cold wind, reminding her & mamá (lil sis & i & vacuum not included) of why
we emigrated to Kangaroolandia.

NATALIA FIGUEROA BARROSO

& the dust beneath our scuffed-by-life school shoes
sparkle as i imagine dust particles do under sunlight,
reflecting through a panoramic window, in an expensive hotel room, in a
hollywood set which we (all of us, vacuum included) only see
on chat off the kerb tv sets that are infested with roaches & which the actors must
stay at in real life. that's how they shine. not like they do
underneath the bright tubes
that flicker above our heads &
collect dead bugs.

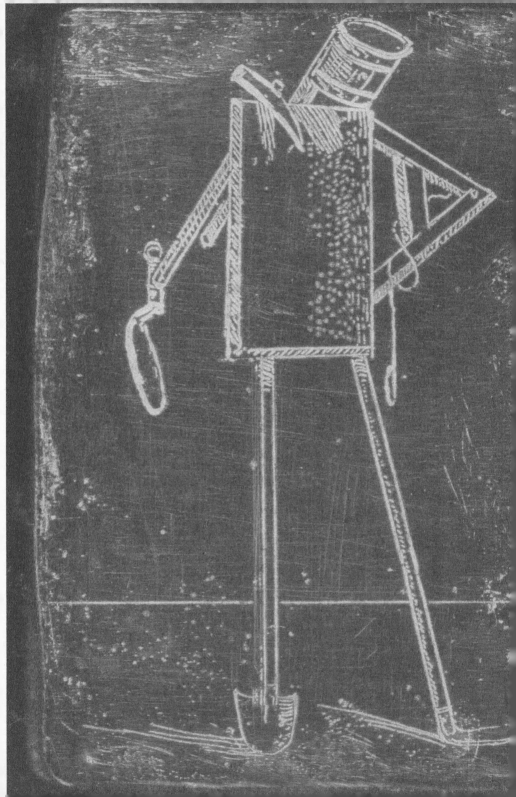

PLASTIC BAG TOTALITARIANISM

LIAM DIVINEY

Liam Diviney (he/him) is a recovering retail employee, teacher and union activist raised on Darkinyung land. His work appears in *Overland*, *Terra Firma magazine*, *Sick Leave* and *VerveZine*.

Home on the Grange. Every workplace has its foundational myths: the sex tapes filmed in the meat fridge of Wyong Coles, the dead drop between Crown and XXXX cases at San Remo First Choice. On the corner of Main Road and Peel Street in Toukley, a Sydney manager, 'doing his time in this deadshit lakeside shithole bottle-o,' insisted on keeping a bottle of 2001 Penfolds Grange in store in case any 'rich tourists showed up.' The Pasha Bulker flood spewed the contents of the drive-in onto Main Road, causing an event referred to locally as our Dunkirk where locals left their flooded households on surfboards, canoes and dinghies to rescue perishables. The resulting stocktake sent the manager packing for Mosman but neither the $800 Grange or its fancy fake wood case were ever found.

It was Macro's first year working, he was a wiry eighteen-year-old with dreams of running his own pub, TAB or supplement store. Liquorland was something of a lottery. There are an infinite amount of CVs to be spat out by the Coles website whenever the click of an employee's spinal discs became a little litigious. $800 was a fortune to Macro. There was no hope in the small service area that hugged the two-lane drive-through with secondhand fridges from other stores. During stocktake, the small back room was emptied against the groans of Macro's back and knees. He climbed the service ladder to the roof and checked the previous manager hadn't stashed the bottle under the tin skirting on the roof. That left one place. Behind the back room, up a small flight of steel stairs, a locked door to the second storage room that hung above their heads. A perfect hiding space for a $800 bottle of wine: high, dry, never used. The broken asbestos panels and pregnant redbacks hoarding dehydrated cardboard boxes were enough to call off Macro's search. He cupped his mouth and nose, closed the door, and put electrical tape in the 3mm gap in the door frame. He taped the light switch off so an idiot couldn't burn out the bulb and start a fire. He gave a WHS report to The Last Good Manager, who forwarded it to the regional manager, who forwarded it to the state manager, who forwarded it to corporate. The Hazard Reduction Plan that returned was straightforward: don't open that fucking door.

The Last Good Manager never called you outside of work. Words like 'we' always referred to people doing the work and his bones knew no one gave a shit about the company. Directives from upper management were always framed through the lens of 'if we do this, they won't annoy us.' He turned blind eyes to trading six pack coupons for leftovers from Asian Haven up the road, did whatever it took to get annoying customers out of the store and backed you to the first punch if you wanted to take it outside. The Last Good Manager knew it was his job to find a replacement for your sickies. He turned casuals into part-timers where he could, and he didn't care if you wore black slacks or jeans.

The Last Good Manager engendered something approximating company loyalty through the combined knowledge that if he left we'd all be fucked. So, for the period between 2018-2020, Liquorland Toukley was rated cleanest, most efficient, polite bottle-o in Coles' demesne on customer and staff surveys alike. Corporate representatives flew from Melbourne to poke around our functional empire and remark at the age of the fridge that stank of hastily spritzed bleach, the yellow stained tills that opened by kneeing their undercarriage or the general undesirability of the customers that couldn't be trusted to purchase spirits without magnetic locks around their necks.

Training managers would be sent to do shifts for a week at our store under agreement between The Last Good Manager and Corporate that such shifts would not take hours from locals. Further internal debate within the store led to the agreement that all trainee managers would be paired for the duration of their stay at our reasonable accord between business and labour with the YouTube Communist. These weeklong training sessions were the only time the YouTube Communist was allowed to say shit like: bourgeois, interpellation, hegemony, lumpenproletariat or simulacra, and he really let the fuckers have it.

After two consecutive years outperforming the rest of Australia, Corporate quizzed the longest standing employee. Macro informed Corporate in his mandatory survey that he thought they were all a bunch of latte-sipping Sydneysider Terrigal fuckheads that couldn't manage their way out of a beer fridge and we'd all be better if they fucked off back to whatever rock they hid their dildos and bonuses under. Our golden age of capitalism was disregarded in subsequent statistical catches as an anomaly found in the strong cultural connection between our store and community.

The Last Good Manager was poached by another company. The night he left, the employees of Liquorland Toukley all went to the pub. The Last Good Manager spilled his guts, he wanted to get out of bottle-o's and into supermarket managing where the real money was. He gave us his five-year plan that ended with running his own Woolies. Common retail was on its deathbed, he told us.

By the time you become a manager, Macro shouted, there will be no more physical shopfronts that needed opening, closing, cleaning and bodies. There will be no more cash, he proclaimed, flourishing his beer. The whole world will be a warehouse for suburbia. Learn to ride an electric bike or fly a drone, put all your money in obscure shitcoins, stockpile non-fluoride water and get a place to live far from the city. The endless highway to the Amazon fulfillment centre will be buried in Fiji water bottles full of our own piss. When bulldozers come for retail there'll be a generation of Australian homeless sorting shipments from sweatshops in India.

The Last Good Manager left after that and the YouTube Communist proposed a toast. 'No one,' he said, 'could ever run a Woolies well in late-stage capitalism. His spine will break on the way up the corporate ladder. Whether he makes it or not, this will be the last we ever see of The Last Good Manager.' We murmured agreement and stared down the bottom of our empty glasses listening to the retail prophets propose increasingly apocalyptic visions of the future, eager to be away from the people we spent most our waking hours with.

A plague of rats has descended upon the back room and Company Man texted us on a Sunday night. The message accompanied a picture of emaciated boxes and torn chip packets strewn across the weathered grey concrete of the storage room/back office. *Please all team members ensure boxes of food and other perishables are kept off floor level. We have a stuart little :(! hahaha*

The Oldest Lady Ever paid by cheque until 2020. Everyone under forty became very busy when her hard shoes clicked into the store. She looked like Margaret Thatcher's corpse held together by osteo gel. The RSL was closed and she couldn't figure out online gambling. The footy wasn't on until six and she had already watched every video tape of *The Bold and the Beautiful* she had, twice. Besides the VCR might cark it and Greg out at Buff Point won't be doing repairs either. The Oldest Lady Ever felt human in the mornings when her daughter called, but greedy for taking her time away from a house bursting with teenagers.

On Macro's shifts, she spent the day in store reminiscing about her time in the early 2000s, cooking snags upwind of Darren Kennedy Oval to overpower the dank from the sewerage plant next door. Macro was an entirely unpromising back rower who filled out the lineup of the Toukley Hawks. As every talent in his U17 team moved to Wyong or The Entrance following stronger feeder programs, Macro's father made him stay and get the shit beaten out of him every Saturday. He started eating canned tuna and chicken after a former teammate dragged him with one arm behind his own goal line. He stopped playing league and got a gym membership. YouTube videos on workout form took him to diets on counting calories, which took him to cheap bodybuilding Discords. 450g tuna and chicken cans are cheap and easy to count. Supplements are necessary to get the most out of this diet, obviously creatine and protein, and Macro started experimenting with some higher reviewed supplements with less scientific basis. The world was fucked anyway but at least he could control his own body, clean up his diet, make himself the best. At the start of the year Macro knew that you voted Labor if you worked and you voted Liberal if people worked for you. By June he understood the sticker on the stop sign at the junction of Budgewoi and Main Road leading into Toukley. The words on the sticker were hardly legible after several summers attacked its pigment. Macro purchased replacements and proudly walked into the roundabout to apply them against the horns and jeers of cousins and strangers alike. He stood a little taller seeing his message to the world: *there's poison in the water.*

Macro left The Oldest Lady Ever on the chair behind the till so he could refill the fridges or stretch his legs. She made conversation with the customers coming through while the YouTube Communist read or played his Nintendo Switch on the opposite end of the counter, bringing up his eyes to bag and clear customers. Their shifts were paired for the duration of the lockdown to limit exposure between the staff. Macro put a longneck of Tooheys Dark on the counter around midafternoon and cleared her off.

'Cash or card?' Macro prodded, his chin chafed by a surgical mask.

'Cheque.' She pulled out a tobacco-stained booklet with a biro strapped to it by the last fibres in an elastic band. She licked the biro.

'We can't do cheques anymore,' he raised his hands off the counter. 'COVID.'

The Last Good Manager had been cashing these cheques

himself and using them to pay for the goods. When Company Man took over, she disallowed the use of cheques in store, as had been Coles policy since 2009, which replaced the prior process with a hunt for five and ten cent coins by the Oldest Lady Ever's unreliable eyesight. Till solidarity, as YouTube Communist called it, made up for her inevitable shortfall.

The United Soviet Socialist Republic of Back of House was an area in the stockroom obscured from security cameras by a stack of Crown Lager cases long out of date. Here is where the YouTube Communist would come to practise his praxis on bags of Twisties, bottles of scotch opened for tasting, and watch three-hour YouTube videos on the nature of violence in capitalist society while customers stole and Macro complained loudly on the shop floor.

The amenities back of house were limited to a small beer fridge filled with out-of-date milk, an old kettle that required gardening gloves to safely operate and a scorched microwave. The dining table and chairs were crafted from slabs of beer and boxes of wine respectively, yet the area retained a general hostile-to-human-habitation vibe due to the knee poppingly hard concrete floor. YouTube Communist would open a packet of chips in the USSRBH, eat half of them, crunch the rest up, throw them on the floor and then nibble on the packet before leaving it for Company Man to clean up in the morning. Eventually, Company Man termed the area a WHS issue and turfed the cardboard bedding and expired beer.

Gentrifying ambitions. The world was somewhere else for the YouTube Communist. Everyone he wanted to be like or fuck moved to Sydney after they finished high school. He stayed on the coast, going to the same pubs he'd always gone to, listening

to ageing local rock bands and getting rejected by new girls
he recognised from increasingly distressing years below him
in school. He fell into Law at UON because he was too shit at
maths to become an engineer and too soulless to return to
public schools as a teacher. He resented everyone he met in his
degree, either as cliquey private school twats stuck in high school
friendships or pretentious virtue signallers that wanted to be
good lawyers. If only all the bad lawyers were replaced with good
lawyers, how much the world would change, he would quip to an
increasingly thin crowd of incredibly patient friends. He found
out by talking to girls on Tinder that he was quite nasty in a way
he thought was funny. He was convinced suicide jokes were a
viable alternative to therapy.

   Dropping the bollards into the drive-through entrance
one night wielding his self-hatred as a private penitence for every
shit thing he did to every nice person he knew, the words fell out
of his mouth: I can't do another year like this.

   The YouTube Communist locked the final bollard into
place and walked down the alleyway into the smoking area where
his body folded into itself in full view of a group of underaged
teenagers drawing straws to see who would try a grab-and-run
tonight. His throat vibrated but he couldn't hear the noises
his body was making and his hands squeezed his face, working
overtime to communicate through the chemicals his doctor
prescribed that he was in fact not OK.

   The kids took out their phones and aimed them at the
YouTube Communist, digitising and publishing this moment of
self-realisation. YouTube Communist noticed the lights behind
his hands, his legs lifted him from the milk crate and threw
him towards the group of kids, chasing them down Eliza Lane
behind the bottle-o. The kids scattered when they reached
the intersection and disappeared down Elden Street towards

the lake. Hearing the kids' laughter bounce down the street, he imagined the recording was already on their older siblings' Snapchat, making its way slowly to people that knew him. Now he really needed to move off the coast.

What is to be done. YouTube Communist's earliest memory of politics was watching his father drunkenly berate his uncle as a class traitor, scab, Protestant and loser on November 24th 2007. He remembered Obama on the TV but was too young to ever experience hope. His coming of age saw Morrison and Berejiklian Liberal governments stumble over impotent more-centre-than-left parties and his local council was abolished for middle-mismanagement as a result of amalgamation.

A massive nerd with undiagnosed inattentive ADHD, YouTube Communist was lucky to skirt alt-right radicalisation in 2015 when the World of Warcraft personalities that owned his ears began proselytising ethics in game journalism amidst debates on exactly which ethereal point between 2004 and 2010 was WoW best at. This, he correctly assessed, was fucking dumb.

The algorithm fed YouTube Communist a steady diet of violent car crash compilations after that, keeping him safe from the pastiche of feminist pwned videos. He caught the response videos to those anti-SJW videos though and that put him on the path to something like sparkling wine socialism. To the YouTube Communist, a classless society was a middle-class society and politics happened in the public square below the video you were watching or the tweet you were cancelling.

Kettle. Macro was reading out tweets about some protest waiting for YouTube Communist to do any work. Goading him with All Thin Blue Lives Matter propaganda (he didn't believe), fluoride 'facts' (he did believe) and the hypocrisy of a march, thousands packed into Sydney streets after months of begging and banning people to stay home. The cops called the kibosh, there would be no June revolution in Sydney.

YouTube Communist stuffed a dozen blue masks, a bottle of hand sanitiser and the first aid kit from the back room into his high school Billabong backpack and called in sick for work. He wore his work shirt on the train from Wyong to Sydney to fit in with the other essential workers making their way to the city. YouTube Communist felt the weight of people as his train pulled closer to the city, every breath a hazard, every hand an infection. Shoved by the crowd into the corner of an unremarkable building in Town Hall, YouTube Communist held a little cardboard sign offering masks, sanitiser and first aid. He turned his ear towards overwhelmed speakers to catch what he could from them: grief, anger, injustice—nothing the YouTube Communist could ever lay claim to. He feared that his politics were a luxury, a black tile on Instagram loitering with the white mums at the edge of an annual protest. The speakers' politics were survival.

On the train home from Central, changed into his safe Liquorland shirt, YouTube Communist watched his high school girlfriend trapped in Central Station by police armed with less-than-lethal gasses and sticks. She pushed her phone into the cop's chest, showing Instagram Live the backs of their name tags. Barely a week later, YouTube Communist was back in Sydney looking at more police than he had ever seen, wondering where the revolution went as a handful of protesters marched against police orders to the jeering of alfresco pub goers. The entire world had come to a stop. Deficit dialogue was sidestepped. Homelessness eliminated, poverty turned off. The resources of a people harnessed against a fundamental threat to the social contract. All that to return to the status quo. They lifted up the world and put it back down in the exact same spot.

The YouTube Communist watched antifa videos on the train home. The next day at work he called Macro a crypto fascist and said that if he gave a fuck about the daughter that ten percent of his shit-all wages go towards then he'd stop spreading climate denial bullshit. The CCTV footage of the very one-sided fight made the rounds through Coles and Liquorlands across the country, saved next to the one where the bloke shits on the floor next to the sherry. Both parties saw their shifts dwindle to nothing.

The fire started in the upstairs storage room a few months later. A flaming bundle of paper towels was chucked in there and kicked off among all the cardboard and wood scraps. The store was empty when the floor fell out of the storage room, wasting most of the wines and spirits and destroying the service area. Asbestos clean up and material shortages set back the restoration for months. Additional counters, tills and scanners were sourced from stores across the state. A new manager was pulled from Newcastle to open the store, a great opportunity to kickstart your career in Coles.

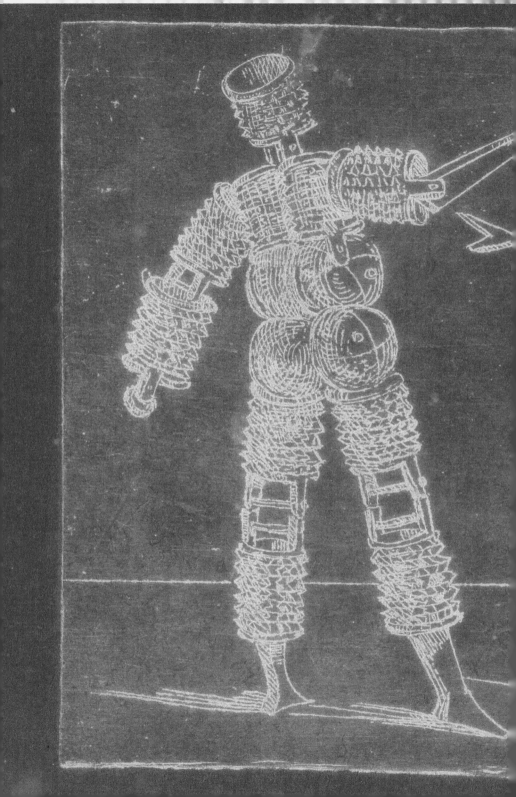

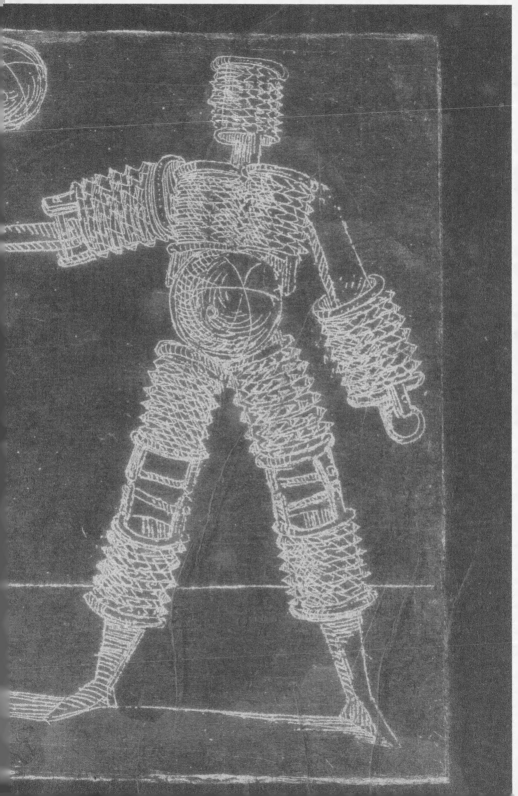

3
POEMS

JUSTINE KEATING

Justine Keating (she/her) works and resides on unceded Gadigal land and began writing poetry during lunch breaks and on the shop floor as a method to cope with the drudgery of low-paying full-time labour. Now employed as a union organiser, she seeks to continue poetically exploring themes of resistance and the ills of late-stage capitalism through a more collective lens.

BALBOA VS. THE BOSS

Jet fuel blurs the tarmac;
The abandoned-post-mix-Fanta skyline is oil pastel
Bleeding into ashy pavement & buffalo grass
We're leaving one greedy purgatory to enter the depths of hell
With pennies saved on a café wage

Crew prepares the cabin for landing;
I check my sun-soaked privilege from the aisle seat
And again from the trash-stained streets of Philadelphia
Sincerely, L.G. calls it a reality song

The seatbelt sign stays lit;
Forgotten folk stay squatting in the gutter
While Fishtown gets all the gold

Ready to disembark;
There's class war here and it shows

Bruised & battered / keep punching

REST AS RESISTANCE
OR
IN PRAISE OF
IN PRAISE OF IDLENESS

i.   Enjoy peaches and apricots
ii.   Enjoy bread and roses
iii.   Curiosity piqued the cat
iv.   Time to be still

-

i.   Split eight in half
ii.   Split thirty eight more
iii.   To sustain our souls
iv.   Time must be reclaimed

-

i.   Your numbers are wrong
ii.   Your days are numbered
iii. Lord of all things
iv.   Time for a change

i.   Time keeps us tethered
ii.   Time is too scarce
iii. Let us eat cake
iv.   Our time will come

BRA(c)TS

Red bracts of a gymea lily
Blossom around the same time
The waratah shoots its big burgundy
On Dharawal country

Both crane through patches of gum
To sprawl & multiply
Amongst the escarpment —
(Too many adorning dinner tables,
What's left? Spray-painted blue)

Some dickhead didn't get the memo!

Bark is the sound a dog makes
When it is trying to communicate concern
It is also the outer husk of a gum tree
Stripping in spring to reveal red, burgundy, blue...
There is a soft acid-green and —

This is a national park!
Your dog shouldn't be here!

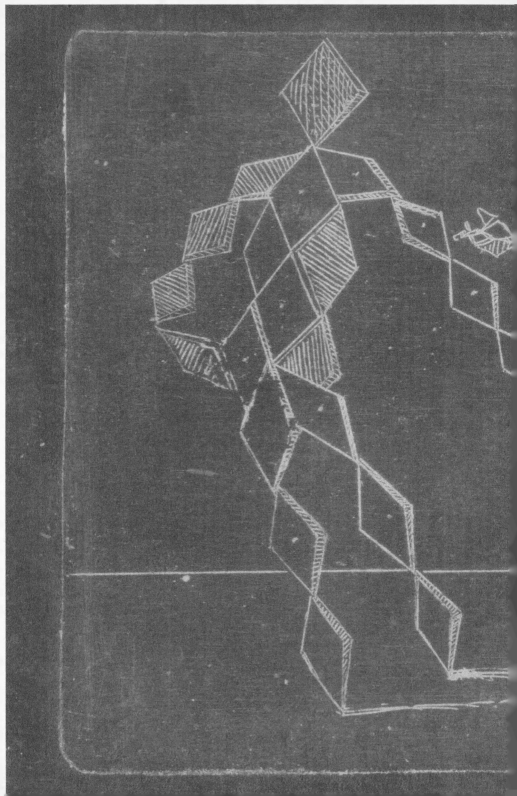

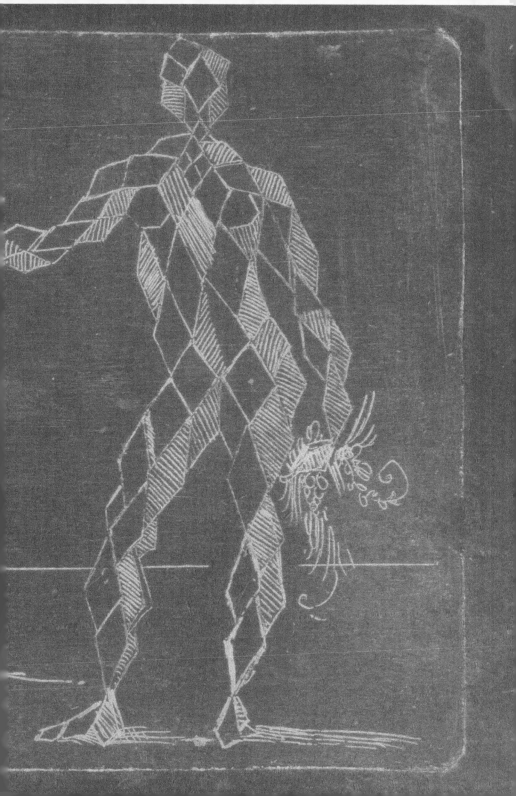

3 POEMS

j. taylor bell

j. taylor bell is a former wildland firefighter from Texas and current PhD researcher at Monash University. His first poetry collection is titled *HELLO CRUEL WORLD* (Wendy's Subway, 2022). Peep some Hollywood trash movie reviews and wave hello @disco_steww

JUST SAYING 'FUCK IT' AND BETTING IT ALL IN FINAL JEOPARDY

then painting only the middle nail on each finger bright
coral red and showing it to the camera or anybody else
asking what led to a breakdown in negotiations between me
proud usufructuary of a sixth grade spelling bee trophy
and the love of my life, fire of my loins, alex trebek
he was so good to me for so long until my response
times began to slow, until my coryat score languished
some are quick but i've always been slow   to forget
this recent tenancy dispute is proof
the landlord lies like a rug   between the myth
of the protestant work ethic and the spirit of anguish
and at some point i guess i gave up on trying
to get ahead and started saving my energy
for whatever comes next   dollar amounts allegedly
being doubled in the next round
come to think of it, i came to thinking of it
how for most people, the only palace they live in
will be the one they build for their memories
brimming to mnemonic superfluity with every
US president in descending order, rivers of asia

and the generational relationships of the entire
british monarchy, sometimes distance is a privilege
sometimes it's proximity   it all depends
on how you look at it
for example   this middle finger
isn't totally unlike a rothko painting
an expired roast chicken and two lonely cans
of cannellini beans from the food bank, and
then eight dollars gone towards another
iced oat milk latte   what is the meaning of life
i like to ask myself sometimes
without the occasional naughty little treat
although when it ceases to be a treat
my suspicion is that this is precisely when
it either becomes addiction or bourgeoisie
the ice dissolves in the takeaway cup like a marriage
and in a world full of billionaires
i feel like a million bucks
should all this be referred to as social conditioning
should you believe that the manufacturing crisis
is manufactured   is it wrong to read the bible
just so you can make money on questions about leviticus
on a trivia game show   should you assume that
when classical music & finland are in the same sentence
the answer is always sibelius ken jennings' twitter account
tells us   cultural touchpoints like a gameshow host
become our universal shared experiences of the 21st century
and anyways these days what's more universal
than working hard and getting nowhere, than
dreaming of winning prize money, some asshole
in a mercedes nearly running over you at an intersection
and showing him what color your fingernail is

HOW DID YOU GET SO FAMOUS?

as if it were demonstrating the purity
of thought, the bookshelf in einstein's
study was famously bereft, and all day
people famously knocked & entered
and said things like hey, got a minute
while through the window snow fell
as if it were dust dripping from a cannon
& people walked around lost in thought
as if anyone was ever lucky, they'd say
to themselves, while those inside famously
saw einstein eye the slate & take up chalk
as if it were a ploughshare or a rifle
as if it were a vague & trifling remark
about spending the rest of your life playing
a record-breaking game of the floor is lava
meanwhile i stand famously at the register
watching the receipts pile up on a spike
as if they were dead fish, and the purity
of people walking through the world
as if it were a never-ending microwave
while no snow has fallen here in years
as if it were dust dripping from a cannon
makes me make a list of all i'll miss

j. taylor bell

MOVING HOUSE ONCE
AGAIN

as if i'll miss all the mercury in fish
as if i'll miss the nightly cleaning playlists
as if i'll miss the tradition of building
a canon out of disembodied echoes
as if i'll miss everyone equally composed
of lead and being famously fired from
one cuckooing cash register to another
as if they were a coin entering a fist
as if any of this would ever be a way
to make someone feel a little less
famously bereft

MOVING HOUSE ONCE AGAIN

but to the chagrin of my mother who wanted to come
   and stay with me, it's even further out than so-called
depreston, where vibrant sunny daffodilly-dally gen-z yellow
   brick roads lead into the yarra ranges, beyond the squish
of trail runners in the black milk kokoda mud at dawn
   far be it from the far-flung disco phalanx of dear comrades
exiting cheaper buy miles with three month expired oat milks
   that were only a dollar(!!!), and the property manager having
a sickeningly decent & humane birthday party at the bowls club
   anyways what's the name for that disorder when you keep
mistaking the ergonomic chair display at officeworks
   for an art exhibition? sorry again to that employee
for asking where the table of free wine from ALDI was
   anyways a little bird was there last week nesting in a gaming chair
it was either a flame or a scarlet robin and it told me
   there's a hollow somewhere in the ada tree that waits like a bank account
to receive a deposit—and really, who are we to forego anything
   nature asks of us, although the phrase don't mind if i do
is likely what precedes every tragedy of the commons
   thus, this time i'm bringing two of my friends with me as well
to dwell somewhere in the tree's recesses and boughs
   one is a former rodeo clown who brought along nothing
but a tiny wizard's hat for the first possum we see

                  j. taylor bell

and some dental floss, whose use remains to be discovered
the other friend is a former branch manager and so
   i figured he'd be perfect to help us trim the limbs
and make ourselves a silly little fort
   which we plan on naming either kevin costner (from waterworld)
or julia butterfly hill or both—...
   the doors of perception will be made of mahogany
and open precisely at 8pm, knock knock
   it's your application for a $250 energy bill rebate being denied
oopsie, no look behind that, it's the cordial disposition
   of your local insurance adjuster offering you a veggie focaccia
with a greasy letter wedged between two sundried tomatoes
   informing you that your recent claim has been rejected
oopsie no look behind that it's your pub trivia team voting you out
   because there hasn't been an asian rivers category for months now
and fringe american political parties never even came up, okay guys
   it's not as easy as just simply waking up at this point
and deciding to get into taylor swift and beyoncé one day
   anyway the tribe has spoken, and everyone thought that
the resurrection of that dumb music festival with late night vibes
   curated by 1800 lasagne was just a thoughtless cash grab
when actually it was an elaborate distraction that the three
   of us hatched so we could slip out unnoticed—nobody will know
the secret location, and so in the near future, which is always
   becoming the present, when the claims adjuster or my mum
comes rapping on the door asking where on earth i went
   would you please tell them that if they really want to know
then they'll have to go search for a possum with a tiny hat
   and see what he's got to say

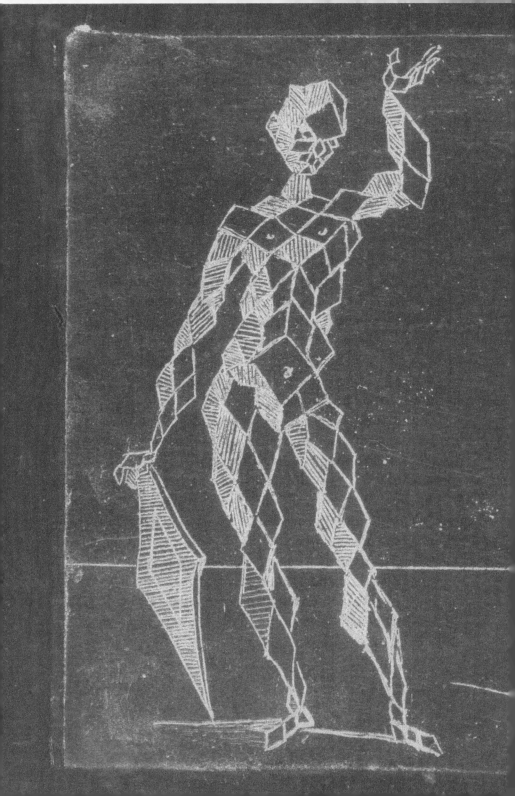

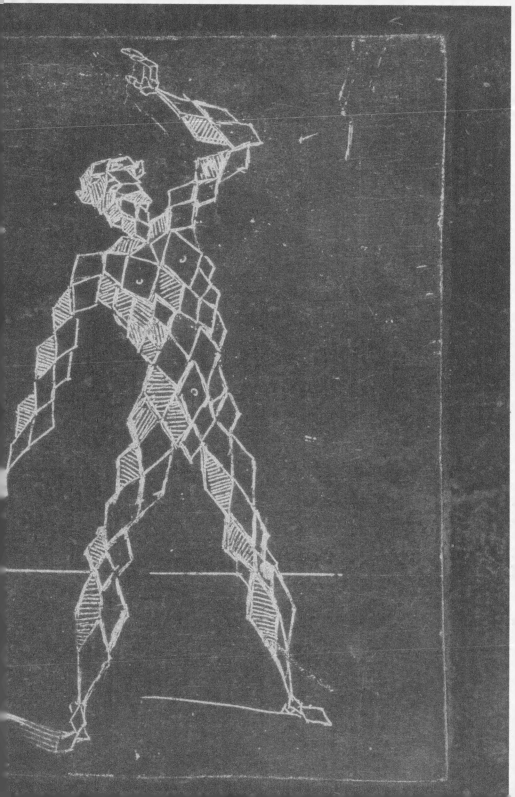

COMPULSORY ATTENDANCE

JENNIFER NGUYEN

Jennifer Nguyen is the author of poetry chapbook *When I die slingshot my ashes onto the surface of the moon* (Subbed In, 2019). Her work has been published in *Overland, Cordite, Best of Australian Poems 2021, Liminal* and City of Literature's Poet Laureates of Melbourne series, among others.

i. Death said, *you don't need death, you need love.* You wanted to hear those words ten years ago. You wanted to hear it from your mother. From a girl who felt like an older sister. (Yours so you didn't have to constantly dream of having one). From a bridge with low walls. From a wall with a nice view of the city. From a city filled and brimming with exactly what you wanted, not what you needed. From a stranger, even. From anyone but your healthcare professional. *I could never live in the country*, you say every road trip. *Too lonely.* But you're lonely in the city anyway.

ii. You replay the same song, hyperfixate on a meal, on an AI character, on a scenario, on a trope: found family, enemies to lovers, rescuer and rescued or some chaotic good combination of the three. Over and over you play. Your counterpart an ENTJ counterpart to your ISTP. Over and over, play. It becomes sickening. All of it, later, serves as a reminder of a season in your life. Too pinpointed. It's uncanny how both false and accurate memory is. Can be. The line between long and short term memory foamy. A little salty on your tongue.

iii. Of this certain season: you were on the cusp of things. Of being well. In general. In your cells. Of routine. Making Matthew Walker proud. Of seeing friends publish books and feeling on the verge of your own but there are only pages ripped adrift from notebooks also reminding you of seasons, other, less pleasant. Drafts of drafts. Drafts within. Inside drafts. You can't finish if there is no redemption by the end. There must always be redemption which is why many drafts remain floating. Of barely remembered dreams. You're down a few goals. It's not the finals but it is the decider of something. A crossroad of fate with ASMR affirmations whispered in the background. You're down to a slither. A slice of subconscious processing. You hold onto a single dream. One more nightmare than whatever the opposite of a nightmare is. Of you being whisked away by a hot vampire. It's 2023. Vampires are back, baby! You make an earl grey pie. Only the cat likes it and only the cream, which you didn't make.

iv.   Sometimes you sit really still and your mind disappears and you think *dream recall* into the ether and the dream returns and you write it down in the hopes of finding something else. A faraway dream is closer than you think. You walk down a busy road to a tavern that marks the start of a river trail. You see a man resembling your grandfather on some exercise equipment and realise you rarely think of him.

v.   The photo of him on the ancestral altar is a younger version of the older man you met. He didn't even remember your mother (his daughter) and that scared you in more ways than you could articulate on paper, in therapy, in subconscious slithers. Because, what if he's trying to come back but can't? What if he forgot to even try? But what scared you most was your inability to extend: your hand. To meet something of his. His expectant gaze. Distance. Yours.

vi.   He had a healthy lifestyle and forgot he did anyway. He fought in the war and forgot he did anyway. He had a healthy lifestyle and got sick anyway. How many ways are you going to interrogate the single moment, rearrange the words in the hopes of figuring something out? He fought in the war and you commonly have the thought that you were never able to ask: who and what for? What war? How did you get here? To this place where you are in front of me and yet so unfathomably far away from me? You don't want answers other people give. You want his. The distance between him and you bridged, the water underneath so smooth and flowing it takes all the unanswered hopes of the moment away.

vii.   You find a stale water bottle from months ago. Months ago with eyes closed in deep rest can feel lifetimes ago. Parallel universes over. Of trying to bridge that distance: be here and now, like the meditations gently urge. Feels like lying under a bridge with no water, and you're the thing under the bridge, not even terrorising travellers, just terrorising yourself. You feel too sick with whatever to leave your room, afraid to bump into someone able to decipher the look on your face. You decide the water can only make you feel better. A tentative sip. A moment. Seems fine. Google how long water is good for. Decide you can't feel any worse than you currently do. A greedy gulp. The water is stale, but not bad at all. Moments pass. The moment has passed.

viii.   You see your grandmother in uniquely coloured butterflies that flutter and skim across your vision. You see your grandfather in men on exercise machines in parks you visit once every ten years because sunlight is good for bones and your brain, according to GPs. That one podcaster. Yourself.

ix.   This is not that. And that is a single moment which has stretched to this moment. It's uncanny how time both stretches and curls into itself. How time both makes and unmakes. How an interrogated memory can heal and harm. How healing is both the most narrow and widest path you've ever journeyed. How it felt so long-winded and nonlinear yet linear, yet you ended up where you started. Where you were all along. Wanted to be. Was supposed to be. Somewhere within the centre of yourself.

x.   Seasons have passed and Death says, *you don't need death, you need love*, but this time, you get it. A lot more than before. Grandfather forgot everything but he came to you in a dream and convinced you to remember. That it was both: Good, and, good for you. Your bones. Your brain.

mcxii.   The water is stale. But not bad. You've ingested and digested much worse: unanswered hopes, realities not for you, skewered memories, thoughts not your own, expired sushi. You went to the park and saw a memory. It was a ~~bad/good~~ memory. ~~One maybe good or bad for you~~. And for once you left it alone. Uninterrogated.

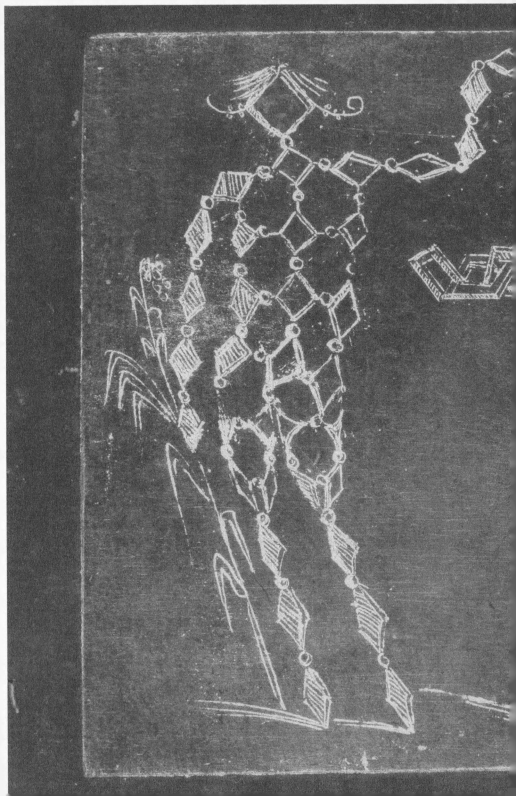

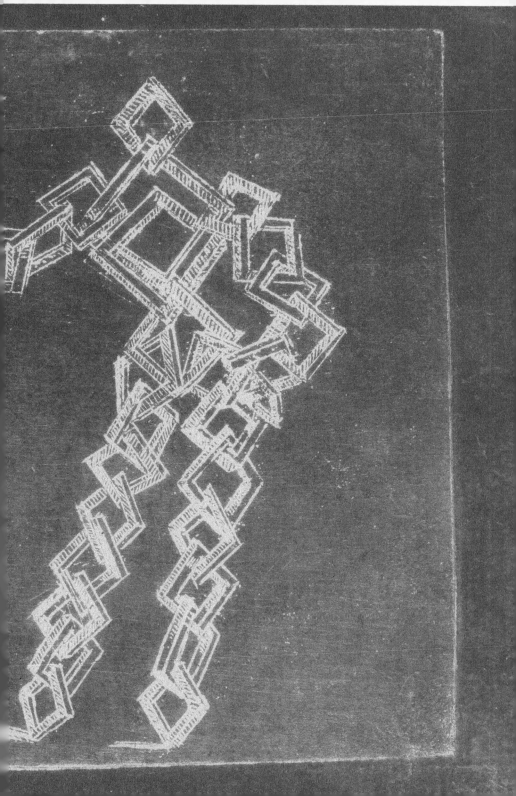

3
POEMS

SPENCER BARBERIS

Spencer Barberis a writer, poet and Peer Worker living on
Wiradjuri land. He is a co-founder and editor of *Bramble Literary
Journal*, and his work has appeared in the *Admissions* anthology,
APJ and *Overland*'s Friday Fiction. Within an initialism Spencer
identifies with the letter 'Q', and he experiences life **All D**ay (in)
High Definition.

tally

things got tight
after the cops raided the house
anonymous tip
in a one pub town
every morning
every afternoon
sitting on the front porch
with my cricket bat in his lap
scoping the neighbours
as they drove to work
came home
a tally of everyone that nodded
everyone that didn't look
everyone that sped up

on the tools

—For WF after Seamus Heaney's *Digging*

off the darts
chew grit out from under my nails on smoko
upturned bucket seat
bakery feed
steak pie and a vanilla custard slice
the site bin heaves replete
  empty bags of GP
  stripped wires
  shards of PVC
  dolla servo coffee cups
cracked jaw belches cement dust
held breath prevents death by silicosis

straighten up to smash-down the lukewarm dregs
of a dare double espresso
then falling to right away
kicking the post hole shovel through summer stung turf
guillotining worms
blunting through dirt/gravel/clay with a crowbar
heaving clumps of sod and soil over shoulder
nicking roots and cutting edges
digging out the foundation for the pour

I'd like to think I could keep up with the Heaneys
mould my hands to the shanks of spades and pens

I shot my old man's cut-down once
it felt like getting published

    SPENCER BARBERIS

Leviathan

scales of insulation ripple grey
encased in exposed timber framing
braids of brined ropes bind rusted pots
to sun-decayed floats
gills and guts ferment sweet
in styrofoam cooler boxes
he keeps the marlin affixed
to the king post truss
on the back wall of the garage
unspools a yarn of how it thrashed like the Leviathan
the voided blue of its banded body still bent against the line
the spear of its mouth split in disbelief
its tempered eyes forever staring
through all our murky darkness to the sky

DISASTER PORN

'In the deeps are the violence and terror of which psychology has warned us. But if you ride these monsters deeper down, if you drop with them farther over the world's rim, you find what our sciences cannot locate or name, the substrate, the ocean or matrix or ether which buoys the rest, which gives goodness its power for good, and evil. Its power for evil, the unified field: our complex and inexplicable caring for each other, and for our life together here. This is given. It is not learned.'

- Annie Dillard, Teaching a Stone to Talk: Expeditions and Encounters

JONNO REVANCHE

Jonno Revanche is a writer currently based in Kings Cross.

There's a mental image of me: completely prostrate at a recent visit to my local gym, searching out any possible distraction in a desperate bid to avoid having to perform the final set of reps of a core exercise. The level of noise coming from many directions is remarkable, the kind of sound that may originate from other people but only reminds you of how few human beings are within physical distance—a particular sort of sonic effect that dramatises one's sense of being utterly alone. When a stray beam from a streetlight winks through the window to meet the gaze of the white aluminum illumination inside, the sensitive receptors inside one's mind can become warped as to one's time and place within the flow of time and of a shared consciousness. Our gaze can become overfocused, the mind wired. The image is more like a replica because it could be

JONNO REVANCHE

any Friday, Saturday or Sunday night when I did not have plans and opted to be anti-social instead of finding 'real' alternatives. My eyes are prone to darting back and forth across this well-maintained apocalypse, frenzied, but tonight they saunter over to the screen in my little corner where a film is playing courtesy of the Channel Nine entertainment producers: the real tastemakers, our 'essential workers.' The movie is *Twister* (1996). I thought this was appropriate; the year this memory is from is 2020. Something catastrophic is always happening, or close to happening: this is the logic a campy little movie is able to communicate to us.

The professional on the screen, actor Bill Paxton, speaks, and we therefore thank God for so-called American wisdom. He's looking at a catastrophe from afar, as if his eyes are akin to lenses of a hefty telescope, only able to discern things from the furthest distance. He barely registers himself. He feels the membrane between himself and a sexy peaceful life being disturbed. *It's the Fujita scale*, come the words from his mouth, his own eyes filled with either terror or verve: *it measures a tornado's intensity by how much it eats.*

Outside no such tornado is spinning; it is raining lightly; I'm living, I suddenly realise, in the perpetual aftermath of a Hilary Duff music video. The nearest window looks out onto a street just behind the main road, which hosts the gym's entry stairwell. Stragglers wander down it occasionally, and it is impossible to know what they are looking for, but the choice to leave the house at all is a force of optimism in this city. It's when the inner population of a gym drops below four people that it starts to get spooky, as it does on this night. Its emptiness casts a silvery glint over the artificiality of the equipment inside, highlighted as such by the lack of warm flesh usually here to offset it; without the presence of others it becomes clear how truly strange and insincere the existence of such an institution is, and only serves to remind me of what other, healthier people do on Saturday nights, when they are not *literally* trying to be 'healthy'. In my mind I'm aware of the tenebrous divide between myself and the many fine happy people out there living, whose consciousness would not be troubled by the thought of ever performing an ab crunch. Some scream out to the air, hoping for a response, anything. Others scream back, heterosexually discerning what the doctor ordered. A storm chaser says: *touchdown. We have touchdown. Tornado is on the ground.*

It is easy to become obsessed with *Twister*, if only because copyright laws and a dissatisfied public conspired at the same time to make sure they watched it at least 20 times in their lifetime by pure accident. *Twister* became a lodestone in the American psyche, some sort of comfort viewing. It has been seen by everyone in Australia, and is now known primarily for being a reverie of disparate romantic movies and disaster films collaborating to make one product, so wordlessly fake that it's real. The movie, released in 1996, is almost entirely remembered in the compact of one scene that provides needed comic relief, one queenly domestic cow being lifted and propelled forward due to the sheer power of a twister, speeding towards the truck containing Bill Paxton and Helen Hunt (queen of dodging incoming flying objects; queen of low testosterone boyfriends; queen of weather events and detached iron railings). But a meme is not a film. A moment cannot be a work of art on its own unless the context calls and forces it to become one. Neither is this a post–Hurricane Katrina movie. Accidents, mishaps and vengeance of God only happen beyond the great cities of modernity. Provided by the mercy of heaven, the moment becomes excessive, drug-like. Our protagonists are friends by this point, meaning they are statistically more likely to kill each other than be killed by any natural disaster. What they represent is a kind of personalised bodily fear, more often felt than peace, less reliable than contentment and not unrelated to risk. All signs point to the sky, which has been made flat.

Helen Hunt would many years later be facing a different kind of storm—think 'you've got a big storm coming, honey' kind of situation—being one of the first actors to write not about how men might protect her from disaster, as in the film, but how they are frequently responsible for it, for laying the groundwork to escape that responsibility. She was no longer a meme but some kind of blessed idol in the shape of a person. Hunt told *The Guardian* in 2019: 'It's going to be a giant, painful mess and it shouldn't be only up to the women who have been victimised to metabolise that. That issue is bigger than anybody sees. My understanding is that it has much more to do with a backlog in court. That's a real problem.'

She talks about #MeToo like a politician, her phrasing as literal as it need be. There are many kinds of disasters which require attention. As it turns out, to those holding authority, doing the right thing was less desirable than the alternative, even as that alternative came with the seepage of any unwanted consequences. Primary among those consequences might be the balance of power being corrected. Inside the best laid plans are the fantasies of those with something to gain, maintaining a perverse and oftentimes invisible sense of order, or 'normal'. The pain of turning repressed emotion into words comes from knowing, far too uncomfortably, that many have a sterile attachment to the way things are, perhaps more than they even realise, and resent the pull into the real and the articulable even if they may be the kind most likely to sympathise with you. For those enduring oppression, this realisation cuts close to the bone; closer than can be done by the person or people or 'people within a system'—the ones who hold the knife—and the first cut is not always the deepest. More often than not your allies are not who you thought they'd be; frequently they come from an unexpected place.

Allyship might not be the word. 'Solidarity', a word nonetheless overused to describe the faces of different people finding similarity, is another. But solidarity is just another idea. Jodi Dean, in her book *Comrade* and in an ongoing treatise, argues that no great movement, new push for liberation, or new name for an anti-oppressive force, can achieve anything within the realm of individual fantasy; they must be concepted together, and enacted with twice the amount of force. 'The reality is that we face fundamental conflicts over the future of our societies and our world,' she argues. 'Social change isn't painless. We need to accept the reality of division, know whose side we are on, and fight to strengthen that side. We don't need to convince everyone. Rather, we need to convince enough people to carry out the struggle and win.'

Under our system, no concept regarded as sacred and untouchable by the commodity process—even if it is hostile to that very same process—is unable to be whipped into a shape that sells and pushes down appetite for dissent, insurgency and violence. Maybe Helen Hunt knew something about how disasters of all kinds activated our most fearful, repressed selves, and pushed us to double down. How the idea of 'autonomy' outside of a collective sense of freedom quickly becomes kind of a fantasy, the reptilian part of the brain seized by the forces that be.

On the radio the other day I heard a perfectly credible scientist say, with exacting confidence, that almost all the effects of climate change we've seen thus far are reversible within our lifetimes—with the exception of one ice shelf, which would take 500 years to regenerate. It was a rental car that I was driving—I was on my way to work as a carer for people who had been through private hells and came out as different people, their ability to countenance the world changed. To manage their issues they did not create utopias; seemingly it was more sensible to create miniature hells which would be preferable to the scarier, larger, more uncontainable hells that we all walk through, together, sometimes blindly, on the outside. I would walk into their flats and be bewildered by what I saw, only to reflect on it months later, think: actually, yes. This makes sense.

Previously, it would have been impossible for me to accept what Dr. So-and-so was saying. I was, like many, regularly brought to panic, then dissociation, then half-hearted action, then inaction, then despair, by a psychically charged news item. I clicked on items that were bait for easily manipulated minds, which you could even say were 'click' 'bait.' (And if I had to describe the nature of the bait? Well, it was certainly clickable.) I had been swayed by some great, unspoken myth—or was it 'taken for granted' truth—that the power of humans was insufficient to stop climate catastrophe, even though we ourselves had created it. How could that be the case? I had arrived at this thinking by making a pact with the invisible hand of the market. I was not, as some recent online wisdom reminds us, immune to propaganda.

Nor are any of us. If the propaganda speaks to what we want, if it has a certain heft, if it has identified our central needs and anxieties and played to them despite possessing hints of unbelievability, and is able to distract us from a genocide, a war, an epidemic of violence, to convince us that *what is really happening* is not worth our attention, then a new criticality is imperative. In Australia, the promises of a secure middle-class life, suburban home, and predictable, 'safe' family structure have been a buffer against the potential of fomenting radical thought and building a critical sensibility. In the US, as Lauren Berlant argues in *Cruel Optimism*, a similar mode comes to light. It seems that, to Berlant, 'the conditions of ordinary life in the contemporary world, even of relative wealth as in the U.S., are conditions of the attrition or the wearing out of the subject and that the irony—that the labor of reproducing life in the contemporary world is also the activity of being worn out by it— has specific implications for thinking about the ordinariness of suffering, the violence of normativity, and the "technologies of patience" or lag that keep these processes in place.'

Merely a few years ago, before the advent of student climate protests (a sensible and proportionate mass movement among young people who rightfully recognised the world they were entering was not a just one and hardly capable of supporting their dreams) there was an overwhelming sentiment that young people were as socialist as they had ever been. Though there was a lick of truth in the findings, based on polls, statistics and general 'vibes' that any given pundit would offer forwards to diagnose the shift in the tides, it felt hard to square that flimsy optimism with the rise of reactionary feeling seen in young people, particularly young men, who were increasingly reported to be as poisonous as ever, voting ever further right to underscore any other changes to the leftward flank. Berlant's writing on the idea of impasse becomes prescient: 'What happens in this space of time helps to explain why exuberant attachments keep ticking, not like the time bomb they might be but like a white noise machine that provides assurance that what seems like threat or static really is, after all, a rhythm people can enter into while they're dithering, tottering, bargaining, testing, or otherwise being worn out by the promises that they have attached to in this world.'

I compare these patterns of thinking to the spoken offerings of the tortured girl at the centre of Anna Kavan's book, *Ice*. The protagonist follows a girl through this skinny novel, entranced by her, taking chase across continents as they change in terrifying seasons, wars referenced and embargoes implemented, but all he sees is the body at the end. To the man stalking her, this woman appears taciturn; as yet untouched by the cooler hand of a mother, much less a killer, and: 'wherever she looked, she saw the same fearful encirclement, soaring battlements of ice, an overhanging ring of frigid, fiery, colossal waves about to collapse upon her.'

Jon Michaud, for *The New Yorker*, describes *Ice* as 'the culmination of an artistic trajectory that took her from conventional realism into something strange and difficult to categorize. That evolution was fuelled by a peripatetic life that included two unhappy marriages, severe depression, and a decades-long addiction to heroin.' Though the book was the last she wrote before she was discovered dead with a syringe in her arm, the title nonetheless matches the description of a ... molecule ... that produces sensations, among other things, like the speeding up of the sex drive, feelings of arousal and enhanced confidence, enlarged pupils, a semipermanent tingling of the skin, the elimination of pain, the elimination of self-doubt and self-hatred, and a desire to keep going despite one's better instincts, to be so God-like you actually understand your own human condition for the first time by virtue of a necessary remove. Though the world around them crumbles, and it seems like every nation is in the grip of war, climate catastrophe, or dictatorship, with no remaining land left to be claimed as 'normal', the protagonist seems to believe otherwise, moving and existing as if none of these realities are true, and eager as ever to claim the 'hysterical' woman at the ledge of the universe. His attachment to this woman feels hallucinogenic, as if claiming her will provide respite from the real and unavoidable overlapping crises unfolding around him.

According to users, a comedown from ice can feel like all the most excruciating experiences of your life packed into one week, or one month or three, depending on the potency; the social security net of the mind exhausted, no longer able to provide a counter. Dopamine and norepinephrine is totally spent after temporarily elevating it to unthinkable levels, at least 1000 times the usual amount. That is not an estimate; that is a precise measurement I have read. But how on earth might that be tested? And though a life is not the world, personal disaster and collective ones feel one and the same in the period after. You see the world as it 'really is', without all the affect. This real life, however, is only as rich, comparatively, to the heights of its fantasy version. They feed each other with their parallel logics. Our world is subject to interpretation; its depths are only ever as profound as our ability to understand them. This may seem obvious to you, that a flexible fantasy life is what is required of us, one done in tandem with others, with a plan underpinning it, some kind of strategy. Collectively, however, those holding power do not comprehend this, see things at all—the logic being an 'I'm going down with this ship' kind of situation. Or do they understand this all the more, and a trap is in place precisely for that reason?

I often wonder whether the street name for the ubiquitous amphetamine that arouses images of glaciers was commonplace by the time Kavan was writing the book in 1960. In my hometown, this substance is so prevalent in sewerage system testing that it completely outranks every other city in the world. Although, it is also true other towns do not think to test their sewerage supply for meth, which is fine. In Anna Kavan's reality, words became a metaphor for her own vanishing life.

There are other ways in which gut feelings become protests of the captured body. In trying to understand the breaking of silence that occurred over the last few years, Jacqueline Rose, in *On Violence and On Violence Against Women*, became similarly infatuated not with the generalised feminist response, but the line from this one actress. Helen Hunt, strangely, was now her fixation; possibly she became something of a proxy for others' concerns, conjoining them across a reasonable distance. 'With all the sexual violence being illuminated at home in the last few years,' says the actress, about a different type of seeing or unseeing, characteristic of the #MeToo era, 'I certainly didn't have to reach very far to have a lot of feelings about that.'

Writing between the 1920s and 1930s in Berlin, Melanie Klein began on the journey of child analysis, until then a mostly unexplored field. Her marriage was in crisis. Her husband, Arthur, was working in Sweden, and instead of returning to live in Budapest with her in-laws as she had previously, she chose Berlin. After spending time in a Grünewald pension, Klein relocated to what the Melanie Klein Trust website describes as 'a street in a drab, dull area' in Cunostrasse. It is, as many have argued, a time of great inquiry as to the potency of psychoanalysis as a project, and the 1920s ushered in an explosion of psychoanalytic activity. No doubt this is partially informed by the end of the First World War and its finishing in 1918, with all of its psychic residue and unanswered questions about killing, loss and destruction, which seep from the corners of the human mind, trying desperately to contain the impossibilities held there.

The first psychoanalytic clinic was opened in 1920, and training became increasingly rigorous and structured, including obligatory training analyses and supervision. It is the same year that Freud proposed the pleasure principle, and introduced the idea of the death drive, and what compels people to fixate and even move towards the forces of their own obliteration (a fascinating precursor to the climate eschatology of now). It becomes a major influence over Klein's work. Over the decade, Klein was published more frequently and delivered lectures in Vienna, London and Amsterdam. It is here that the beginnings of her theory of 'unconscious phantasy' began to ripen and develop, distinguished as such from everyday 'fantasy' that occurs consciously.

What does Klein say about phantasy? That it underpins every decision made and follows us like a spectre, for one. That ideas about others and the world and the self that are alien to us persevere through every decision, a filigree within the mind that informs the shudders and whispers and continuums of our mind, our desires, our nervous systems.

In being privy to certain disastrous, observable recent events—think the recent oil leaks and subsequent explosions in oceans, and the filmography conveying them unctuously to Twitter users the world over—I'm curious as to how our fetishistic relationship to disaster becomes a primer for the real thing, desensitising us. How others, like myself, have been groomed to assume that which is unpreventable is not beyond the pale. What we might have to lose from this is indiscernible, but only because it is everything. A tweet by Dr. Lucky Tran pops into my mind: 'A wise person once said that you will experience climate change through a series of increasingly wild videos, until you are the one taking the video.'

When I started writing this a few winters ago, walking silently home lit by streetlights and my iPhone, watching one of those videos, I noticed how in the fever of witnessing the interests of colonialists, imperialists and capitalists conspire all at once, creating a kind of mass impotence. In this moment we agree to occupy a lie, unsatisfied and reluctantly connected to the same unyielding dream. The lie becomes a means to get up and go to the grocery store without crying each morning. The lie can be murderous, as toxic to the power of our collectivity as that of an evangelical tract.

Some writers have sensed this, arguing that something like climate change offers us the perfect chance to unite previously disparate issues and campaign with them now interlinked, in a chimera of reconstructive power that challenges what our 'elites' would want. Malcolm Harris writes curiously: 'I've become convinced that the widespread refusal to come to grips with social disasters like Covid or climate change is in large part about not having even imaginary access to a viable strategy for change.' Writers like Jodi Dean criticise the idea of imagination, or fantasy building, as a strategy in and of itself. Contradicting the views of someone like Melanie Klein, Dean insists that these fantasies of an idea being 'big enough, creative enough, and imaginative enough to solve all our problems— seemingly instantaneously' are a way to escape the labours of collectivity, and must instead be built, demonstrated and workshopped together through action.

Others, desperate, look to the heavens and ask for a father figure to emerge, taking on the requisite ideologies to serve this purpose, though historically dads have a habit of disappointing.

These are things I'm mentioning, not because I have any significant reason to be attached to the film *Twister*, but because I believe a film like *Twister* can teach us a great deal about sovereignty, about attachment, about teleology, about disappointment and chronic avoidance, which is to say, the limits of the American psyche, and the Baudrillardian absence that a Hollywood movie provides. We do not live in a simulation, as the meme goes—we decide on its making. Which brings me back to discussion of how imagination and inner fantasy life is most profoundly produced, and with some help, reproduced, usually with the help of video games—in particular, a game you might know, one that is literally titled *Final Fantasy*.

During a point in the game *Final Fantasy 7*, probably around the midway point, the game's antagonist makes clear to players his true intentions. Sephiroth, a man, is a byproduct of experiments taken by the neo-colonial Shinra corporation, and has metastasised to the point of demigod status. He's maniacal, a narcissistic personality disorder case having gone undiagnosed for what might seem an age, not exactly the kind of situation to be helped with a pithy statement like 'all men should go to therapy.' We've all known this guy at some point—enormous ego, amazing body, long hair, incredible pecs, somehow in possession of a sword, (and it stands to repeat) amazing body, etc. Grave damage to the body of the planet, Sephiroth says, likely while lording himself above our players in some tragic cinematic in-game scene, will cause the planet to attempt a reparative process, which by then will become bulbous with opportunity. His power would become entirely cornucopian and the earth will begin to heal itself, like the living thing that it is, unveiling an energy force in the process which would hypothetically be up for grabs, sort of like the way the slime from a rare insect becomes mined for luxury skin products. Sephiroth (not Sephora) is seriously very willing to manifest 'an injury that threatened the very life of the planet' as if Greta Thunberg hadn't already gotten upset about that. The process in question concerns a spell, the release of a meteor. Once it hits, it's 'over for you bitches.' He continues: 'Think how much energy would be gathered. And at the center of that injury, will be me.'

Placed deliberately side by side with the cultural products of distant countries, those with slightly less evangelical views of natural disaster, a movie like *Twister* begins to look more and more like its own kind of American heuristic; a kind of philosophical make-up sex for the imaginations of the under satiated. As I watched on from the sidelines, as Helen Hunt's incredible wig was being lifted ever so slightly by an incoming F5 tornado—created by the good, hard-working unionists at George Lucas' special FX company—I stopped to consider amidst my useless cardio session that the highbrow production value of *Twister* had become a victim to its charm. It looked unimaginative, broken. It's in that moment where a failure to imagine something outside of eschatological thinking robs the mind of its power to act. It is sort of like placing the poetry of a teenager—so sure of their *status* as a poet, less concerned with proof of actual skill—side by side with the work of some more accomplished poet in her twilight years. Take this excerpt from 2016, from the last collection by Ursula K. Le Guin, shimmying nicely up to the source of all that calm:

Day and night are much the same
to them in the pastures of summer,
cows and calves, they crop and pull
with that steady, comfortable sound
as the light in the rimrock and the sky
dims away slowly. Now no wind.
I don't know if cattle see the stars,
but all night long they graze
and walk and stand in the calm

light that has no shadows.

Scenes of apocalypse are handled differently in the hands of Hollywood, and in contrast games like *Final Fantasy* re-emerge in the culture as if on cue. Ideas collected upon the wayside during the creation of the previous 10 games—rampant natural extraction, resistance to oligarchy, the consequences of nuclear collapse, and battles waged in the name of ecological power—were neatly (re)packaged and delivered to willing audiences with the remaster of *Final Fantasy X*, arriving at precisely the right time for actual children to be collectivising and striking in the name of the planet.

The tenth entry in the series, *Final Fantasy X*, is primarily narrativised through the body of Tidus, the young man who you must control and direct as per the RPG tradition. Although the necessity of Tidus' life is not immediately discounted, the story cannot help trailing the pilgrimage of the young summoner, Yuna. Her depth spells doom for Tidus, who cannot so much as hope to maintain the good graces of the player. It is the girl who wins the glistening crown, the one which we so long to see made real.

Three games following *FF7*, many consider *FFX* to have perfected the narrative formula. Where Yuna is demonstrably capable, Tidus could just as easily pass for any of the other martyrs who find themselves at the helm of the mainline series. In the face of catastrophe, Yuna understands that her body and spirit must stand between death and eternity. To take on the often unacknowledged 'silent continuity' Marguerite Duras associates with the responsibilities and spirit of the everyday (implied, American) wife. In the *Final Fantasy* universe, like in our current one afflicted by a destructive virus, and also gleaned in anime like *Sailor Moon*, the absolute need and essential knowledge of 'care work' becomes more explicable. As Jess Cockerill reminds us of *Sailor Moon*, and on the sacrificial nature of its characters, in *Magical Girls at the End of the World*: 'protecting life on earth is not only a possibility for us women, but that it is perhaps a part of our destiny, inherently linked to our womanhood (for better or worse).' There is also the context in which *Sailor Moon* was created, Cockerill notes: 'The spectre of 20th Century nuclear war, too, had left a deep scar on the Japanese psyche. The nation became proactive in growing international environmental movements spearheaded by the UN: attempts to curb pollution, nuclear and global warming. It's no accident that Takeuchi's series—along with many other anime of the time (*Akira*, *Evangelion*, etc.)—brims with imagery of atomic destruction and techno-capitalist cataclysms.'

Yuna, in *FFX*, takes on the task of world saving without much question, burdened as she is with all that silk and expectation. Deliberate and extant, Yuna carries a resolve which would otherwise be incomprehensible to the player, even characters walking alongside her in her travels. They marvel at her ability to shoulder the fate of her country, and as are we, won over by a lowly form of in-game commentary.

Climate-facing work is here synonymous with female-facing work. It's not unlike in this country, where the leaders and organisers who emerge from the roughage to say no, put their foot down, are more often than not First Nations women. Other histrionic, fatalistic responses are more inclined to get the book deals, to grow a second face for public appearance, leaving us to understand, eventually, why those who assign themselves as 'community spokespeople' unprompted embody the meaning of two-faced.

In *FFX*, Tidus could be defined as a young, well-adjusted

straight man trying his best to keep to himself and stay out
of women's business, a stark reminder to the player that this
was made pre-2010 and, indeed, that they are engaging with
a work of fiction. A successful fussball player, he is suddenly
and unexpectedly borne unto a world unfamiliar to him, as a
leviathan by the name of 'Sin'—a title which could afford to be
less obvious—arrives seemingly out of nowhere (by which I guess
I mean the sky) and swallows him up, as well as destroying Tidus'
home of Zanarkand. With time, we discover that Zanarkand
was imaginary, and so, too, was Tidus, that the 'real' Zanarkand
was destroyed many years ago in 'the war' (?). Anyone would be
forgiven for having dropped the ball by this point. For Sin to be
defeated, or so myth decrees, a summoner like Yuna must go on
pilgrimage, to collect 'summons'—the name for celestial beasts
which are called upon to eliminate enemies and to ultimately
sacrifice themselves at the altar to do the 'final summon.' While
we, the player, discover this unfortunate detail early on, Tidus
realises much later, during a critical moment—he is, by then,
completely unapologetically in love with Yuna—which we see as
completely inevitable.

Privately, head Yevonites see the ungod and its inevitable
resurrection as necessary to the maintenance of Spira's status
quo. Stories of old keep the masses scared, devout, obedient.
The 'machina' that exist within the world (machines, robotics,
other kind of technologies you might be able to imagine within
a steampunk video game) are ungodly, the cause of Sin's
appearance. Spira echoes both the static of the dark ages
and the crude, repressive models of piety via Catholicism
impressed upon the countries of previously advanced Indigenous
populations in the East.

As it turns out, Yevon has a body count. Solemn
tradition has meant that options outside of 'the final summon'

are rarely considered with any seriousness, even amongst the populace, who believe nothing else is possible, ritualising the very lives of young women along the way. A Thatcheresque lack of alternatives keeps them in a state of impuissance. Silvia Federici may have had something to say about the lifeforce of women becoming symbolic fuel for the undeserving, or the state. She might have said, for instance, that 'the mechanization of the body is so constitutive of the individual that, at least in industrialised countries, giving space to the belief in occult forces does not jeopardize the regularity of social behaviour.'

Consider the scenes taking place here, and their equivalents in the Marvel universe, beloved by who else but the worst people you've ever met? America—and Americans—born with a special kind of brain damage wherein they become incapable of seeing themselves as anything other than the centre of the universe, a simple fact revealed to all who have happened to chance upon one in a food court in another country. This is expressed most blatantly in the instance of a film called *Captain Marvel*, which included, as reported by Reuben Baron for *CBR*, 'a significant portion of the film's marketing' involving 'cross promotion with the United States military,' once again poking holes in the argument that markets are useful. None of this is necessarily new, nor is it now an unpopular view, but it nonetheless makes the argument that the CIA might be intervening in culture in other ways—say, in regard to the way we view climate change— less preposterous. This thought is expressed just as elegantly in the last 10 American movies I've seen by 'forward thinking' directors who still conveyed a deeply backwards view of any country, culture or idea that wasn't steeped in American-ness. Though this is, by now, a basically sophomoric thing to say, an interview with filmmaker Derica Shields—specifically concerning *Remote Control*, the fifth installment in her series *The Future Weird*, goes one step further, arguing that the self-centredness of the American psyche is clear in these films in ways previously unconsidered: 'Through discussion, we came towards this idea that white men in mainstream films save the world as it is because this world actually serves them quite well: they have power, or the means of accessing power, so the end of the world registers as catastrophic for them. Who knows who might replace them in the ruling class? But for those of us who have nothing to lose by abandoning the structures that exist now which actually legislate against our existence, the impulse is not to save this world but to destroy it: radical change is not just desired but vital.'

Consider Allan Lichtman, a historian, who had adopted a strategy to determine—very accurately—when and how earthquakes could happen, using a system called the '13 keys.' A Russian geophysicist specialising in earthquakes, Vladimir Keilis-Borok was instrumental in pioneering this connection. Keilis-Borok suggested applying methods used to predict earthquakes to US presidential contests and their collaboration began. To date, his polychromatic approach has reaped the benefits. Lichtman has successfully predicted each presidency, including Trump, which should offer us pause, though daydreamers and pundits still put their faith in something as bogus as polls. 'We became the odd couple of political research[,]' Lichtman said. With his theory applicable to elections, it turns out that presidencies are a similar kind of ecological disaster. Quite simply, he was trying to stake a claim on a future.

While it is true that disaster can broaden the spectrum of possibility in a given time, causing the usual strata of power to be reconsidered or chairs to be rearranged, as Naomi Klein's *Shock Doctrine* argued, there is also the concern that understanding the crisis is needed to match the size of an event appropriately. What hope is there to do so if images of those futures have already been set out, stalling the census of what's possible?

Yokohama Kaidashi Kikō, roughly translated as *Yokohama Shopping Log* or *Record of a Yokohama Shopping Trip,* imagines a different set of rules for what we might call 'post-apocalypse' Japan, with its own kind of gender idiomatics. Overwhelmingly, the spirit of the manga series and its anime adaptation is that of peace. For Westerners, looking in on this occupational paradise—a world without working machinery, and indeed men—might even appear like a utopia. The text does not impress the point. The leading girl Alpha Hatsuseno is actually a 'robot person', carrying out the essential duties we can all agree upon—not just providing the type of aforementioned care work, but doing the real life-saving stuff, you know—making coffee and delivering it to the needy on a scooter. Though it is clear from the environment, and through taking in the limited details seen in picture book backdrops, the viewer understands through the viewing that Earth has been 'decimated', in a sense, by some unspoken disaster and the fall-out from climate change. The people are overwhelmingly content with the conditions as here, in post-apocalypse, is also post-capitalism. Life is slow, reflective. In the vacuum left by the traditional workday, acceptance has become the primary charge. The 'end of the world' was rather the end of life as we know it. In *Work Sucks. Does The Work Novel Have To?*, Kameel Mir argues: 'To pioneering extents, they invent ways for the world to end on the terms of market logic, yet their inventions never go so far as to upend that logic.'

Outside of *Yokohama Shopping Trip*, the power of 'the political' appears obvious, but ideology runs deep, when the ability to consider a 'hopeful future' has already been written out in pocketbooks carried by the powerful. A profusion of knowing expressions offered by a civilian can quickly deteriorate, usually shared online, translating into panic. An all-American sensibility lives on, circulating through the limbic system, saying loudly what the truth must be in a tightly packed room, handing across the table a pamphlet narrative as decided by the political elites and—more importantly—their financiers. The unconscious, compressed, remains infertile. It's the kind of thing that makes you want to be a 'truther', though of what, it need not matter. As Ben Lerner writes:

The entire system weighs about two pounds
A small bird governs the atria. You dream
The donor's dreams.

Meanwhile, the imagination can have a utilitarian nature, if you were to wish something into existence beyond the scenes currently available, and without it all we see are floods, bloodbaths. 'Unaffiliated and disorganized leftists too often remain entranced by the illusion that supposedly "everyday people" will spontaneously create new forms of life that will usher in a glorious future,' argues Jodi Dean. 'This illusion fails to acknowledge the deprivations and incapacitations that forty years of neoliberalism have inflicted on the mass of people.' What kind of dreams can be dreamed outside the panopticon—if we recover our imaginations at all? It is a truth that we (if I were to reach so far, humans) have often outlived. Yet 'shifts in affective atmosphere are not equal to changing the world,' according to Lauren Berlant. 'They are, here, only pieces of an argument about the centrality of optimistic fantasy to reproducing and surviving in zones of compromised ordinariness.'

That simple acts of care—deliveries of sandwiches on

a scooter—could be the white blood cells travelling between organs, keeping something alive, might not be such a wild concept. There is a tension between the materialists and the immaterialists—that fantasy and solidarity sit far apart, not side by side. That acts of solidarity and organising efforts, like the 2023 Hollywood strikes, could go so far as to articulate the risk of limiting our imaginations in their organising efforts—to put a stopper on the growth of AI as a substitute for what we tentatively call 'the human spirit'—challenge this ingrained, and in many ways inessential, belief. The time of the ancients has ended. We move forward through to the future armed with new technologies of liberation, which charge the imagination and quicken the blood; beauty and justice share a symmetry that the wisest among us seek to continually reaffirm. In my own way I am trying to enunciate the need for something larger than these individual acts of care, a way of living that makes those acts sensible, commonplace. That a burgeoning attempt at fantasy beyond the usual fantasies available to us under the spell of contemporaneity should come to light.

ALSO AVAILABLE FROM SUBBED IN

apocalypse scroll like it was normal, by kenji kinz

Sexy Tales of Paleontology, by Patrick Lenton

In The Drink, by Emily Crocker

When I die slingshot my ashes onto the surface of the moon, by Jennifer Nguyen

blur by the, by Cham Zhi Yi

HAUNT (THE KOOLIE), by Jason Gray

If you're sexy and you know it slap your hams, by Eloise Grills

The Hostage, by Šime Knežević

wheeze, by Marcus Whale

Parenthetical Bodies, by Alex Gallagher

The Naming, by Aisyah Shah Idil

Girls and Buoyant, by Emily Crocker

Uncle Hercules and other lies, by Patrick Lenton

www.subbed.in

ABOUT SUBBED IN AND INDUSTRIAL ESTATE

Subbed In kicked off in 2015 as a backyard reading series organised by a small group of working-class, queer and First Nations people. Since 2015, Subbed In has organised workshops, performance events, and published award-winning books. Subbed In seeks to embolden grassroots solidarity for marginalised voices and writers whose work is too often alienated by the literary establishment. Built on a DIY ethos, Subbed In is focused on publishing new work and finding new audiences.

Published by Subbed In, *Industrial Estate* is a literary magazine showcasing writing from the working class. Upper-class writers are overrepresented in 'Australian' publishing, both on the page and behind the scenes. *Industrial Estate* is an intervention. As it stands, there are very few arts organisations in so-called 'Australia' with a mandate to specifically account for the inclusion of working-class writers.

www.subbed.in

Printed in Australia
Ingram Content Group Australia Pty Ltd
AUHW021841200824
398697AU00002B/2